03|17

A Puzzle to
Be Named Later

This Large Print Book carries the
Seal of Approval of N.A.V.H.

A PUZZLE LADY MYSTERY

A PUZZLE TO BE NAMED LATER

PARNELL HALL

THORNDIKE PRESS
A part of Gale, Cengage Learning

GALE
CENGAGE Learning·

Farmington Hills, Mich • San Francisco • New York • Waterville, Maine
Meriden, Conn • Mason, Ohio • Chicago

GALE
CENGAGE Learning®

LIBRARY OF CONGRESS CATALOGING-IN-PUBLICATION DATA

Names: Hall, Parnell, author.
Title: A puzzle to be named later : a Puzzle Lady mystery / Parnell Hall.
Description: Large print edition. | Waterville, Maine : Thorndike Press Large Print, 2017. | Series: A puzzle lady mystery | Series: Thorndike Press large print mystery
Identifiers: LCCN 2016055494| ISBN 9781410497857 (hardback) | ISBN 1410497852 (hardcover)
Subjects: LCSH: Felton, Cora (Fictitious character)—Fiction. | Crossword puzzle makers—Fiction. | Murder—Investigation—Fiction. | Women detectives—Fiction. | Large type books. | BISAC: FICTION / Mystery & Detective / Women Sleuths. | GSAFD: Mystery fiction.
Classification: LCC PS3558.A37327 P793 2017b | DDC 813/.54—dc23
LC record available at https://lccn.loc.gov/2016055494

Published in 2017 by arrangement with St. Martin's Press, LLC

Printed in Mexico
1 2 3 4 5 6 7 21 20 19 18 17

For Yogi Berra,
always a puzzle

THE MVPS

I would like to thank my star player/manager Will Shortz, *New York Times* crossword puzzle editor, for coaching the team to victory and creating the Sudoku.

I would like to thank the speedy Fred Piscop, noted *New York Times* crossword constructor, for creating the crossword puzzles in record time. Coaches still click their stopwatches and shake their heads in amazement.

And I would like to thank everyone's MVP, Ellen Ripstein, the American Crossword Puzzle Tournament Champion, for editing the puzzles, and saving me, once again, from leading the league in errors.

CHAPTER 1

Cora Felton could hardly contain herself. She beamed like the cat who swallowed the cream, batted her cornflower blue eyes. "Matt Greystone," she purred.

Sherry Carter looked up from the stew she was stirring on the stove. "Who?"

Cora's mouth fell open. "You don't know who Matt Greystone is? You're lucky I let you use my kitchen."

Sherry smiled. "Oh, now it's *your* kitchen?"

Cora's kitchen was the one in the old part of the house, the prefab ranch house Cora and Sherry moved into when they first came to Bakerhaven. When Sherry got married, she and her husband added on an addition, a modern two-story affair, which of course had its own kitchen, but Sherry felt more comfortable cooking in Cora's.

"Fine. It's our kitchen, I'm glad you're using it. I'll try to make you feel welcome

9

by eating some of your stew. Don't you know who Matt Greystone is?"

"I'm sure you're going to tell me."

"Only the biggest story to come out of Yankee Stadium in the last twenty years."

"Bigger than winning the World Series?"

That caught Cora up short. "What?"

"It seems to me the Yankees won the World Series a few times in the last twenty years. You mean bigger than that?"

Cora shook her head. "You're not a Yankee fan. I can't believe you're not a Yankee fan."

"We're in Connecticut. A lot of people are Red Sox fans."

"I wouldn't say that too loud if I were you."

"Why not?"

"Matt Greystone!"

"I see. And you were going to tell me who that is."

"Come on, Sherry. This wasn't just a sports story. The guy was on every talk show in America. He's the player to be named later."

"I thought you knew his name."

"Don't be a wiseass."

Jennifer, swooping through the living room in pursuit of Buddy, Cora's toy poodle, stopped and pointed. "Auntie Cora said 'ass'!"

10

"That doesn't mean you get to," Sherry said. "What did I tell you?"

Jennifer made a face, shook her head, rolled her eyes. "Auntie Cora said the A-word."

"That's right. And who's not going to say it in kindergarten?"

"Suzie Bromowitz?" Jennifer said brightly. She giggled, pursued the poodle out the door.

"She's growing up entirely too fast," Sherry said.

"I thought there was a playroom in the basement."

"There is."

"Doesn't she like it?"

"She does."

"How come she's never down there?"

"The grown-ups are up here." Sherry turned back to her stew. "You were saying something about Matt Greystone."

"Yes, I was saying something about Matt Greystone. You really don't know who he is? He's the minor league pitcher the Diamondbacks threw in to complete a trade. Surprised everyone by going seventeen and seven with a three-point-two-one ERA. Yankees signed him to a seventy-five-million-dollar extension, and every sportswriter in the world said it was a steal."

11

"I gather it wasn't?"

"Good guess. Kid celebrated by driving his car into a large tree. Broke his arm in five places. Hasn't thrown a ball all year and probably never will."

"And he's here?"

"He's coming."

"What makes you think so?"

"I don't think. I know."

"How do you know?"

"I have it on good authority."

"What good authority?"

"Judy Douglas Knauer. She's been showing him houses."

"Then why doesn't everybody know?"

"She's not supposed to talk about it. It's very hush-hush."

"Then how do you know?"

"She told me!" Cora shrugged. "Hey, it's not like I'm going to tell anyone."

"You told me."

"You're family." Cora shook her head. "I can't believe my niece doesn't know anything about baseball."

"I know who led the National League in home runs in nineteen thirty-two."

"Who?"

"Mel Ott."

"How the hell do you know that?"

"Ott is a very useful crossword puzzle

word. That's just one of many ways to clue it. As the Puzzle Lady, you should know that."

Cora Felton was the Puzzle Lady in name only. Her face graced a nationally syndicated crossword puzzle column, and she appeared regularly on network TV hawking breakfast cereal to schoolchildren, but if the truth be told, Cora couldn't do a crossword puzzle if her life depended on it. The truth wasn't told, of course, because it would have meant the end of her career. Sherry Carter was the true Puzzle Lady, and constructed all the crosswords for the column. They put Cora's name on it because Sherry was hiding from an abusive ex-husband. The husband was long gone, he and Sherry were both remarried. The pretense remained because the TV ads were lucrative and the public wouldn't like to find out they'd been duped.

"How can you know that and not know who Matt Greystone is?"

"I know who Matt Greystone is."

"What!" Cora cried indignantly.

Jennifer, swooping through in pursuit of Buddy, stopped to watch.

Sherry smiled. "Cora, I'm married to a newsman. You think I don't know who Matt Greystone is? Besides, I have to keep track of all celebrities in case I want to clue a

name that way. His ERA was three-point-
two-*seven*, by the way."

Cora let out an exasperated exclamation.

Jennifer pointed. "Auntie Cora said the
S-word!"

CHAPTER 2

Chief Harper was nervous as a schoolboy. He was all decked out in his dress uniform, which was getting a little tight. The Baker-haven chief of police had put on weight over the years, and never felt the few ceremonial functions that required a uniform warranted a new one. "Do I look all right?"

"Chief. Relax," Cora said. "It's just a picnic."

"It's not just a picnic. I have to make remarks."

"Isn't that the first selectman's job?"

"Yes, Iris Cooper will speak. She wants me to say something, too."

"Why?" Cora said.

Harper gave her a look.

"Not that you're not an excellent choice," Cora said. "I mean, isn't Iris enough?"

"Apparently not. They're pulling out all the stops for this one. I have to get up and make a fool of myself."

15

"You talk on TV all the time."

"Yeah. We arrested so-and-so. We are pursuing leads in the case of such-and-which. That's totally different than spouting ceremonial crap and fawning over a ball-player."

Cora's eyes widened. "Why, Chief Harper. You're starstruck. Totally understandable. After all, it's Matt Greystone."

"I'm surprised they didn't ask you to speak."

"I don't think Matt Greystone does crossword puzzles."

"Yeah, but you're a celebrity. You've been on TV, he's been on TV. It's a natural."

"Iris didn't ask me, she asked you."

"I was talking to Iris. She doesn't want you to feel slighted."

"I don't feel slighted."

"You're a sports fan. Wouldn't you love to meet Matt Greystone?"

"I'd love to talk baseball with him. I'm not so keen on gushing about how flattered our town is he's graced us with his presence."

"Damn."

"What?"

"That's what it's going to sound like, isn't it?"

"Relax, Chief. You'll be great."

16

Officer Dan Finley stuck his head in the door. "Got your speech ready, Chief?"

"No, I don't have my speech ready," Harper said irritably. "I'm not making a speech. Just a few remarks."

"Oh, right," Dan said. "Got your remarks ready?"

"He's rehearsing them now," Cora said.

"Good idea, Chief. Wanna try 'em on me?"

Harper looked from one to the other. "I am *not* rehearsing them now. I do *not* want to try them on you. This is not a big deal."

"Good for you, Chief," Dan said. "I'm amazed you can be so cool. If I had to introduce Matt Greystone on national television, I'd be scared to death."

"It's not national television, it's Channel 8 News."

"Yeah, but it will get picked up by network TV. They'll probably play the clip on the evening news."

The phone on Chief Harper's desk rang.

Dan scooped it up. "Bakerhaven Police Department, Dan Finley speaking . . . Oh, hi, Amanda . . . Really? Well, we'll check it out. Not right away, of course, because we have this picnic, and —"

Harper ripped the phone out of Dan's hand.

17

CHAPTER 3

The Bakerhaven fairgrounds was all decked out with red, white, and blue bunting and banners and streamers and the like, and while it was decked out every Fourth of July, this Fourth of July was something special. Cora noted a hint of pinstripes in the decorations, the number seventeen woven into the motif. She would not have been surprised if the high school marching band, a Fourth of July staple, had expanded its repertoire to include "Yankee Doodle Dandy."

The fairgrounds, an idyllic, grassy meadow sloping down toward the river, had never, at least in Cora Felton's memory, had a fair. Bakerhaven had no livestock, traveling carnivals were prohibited, even the crafts fair was held outside the church. In fact, half the town referred to it as the parade grounds, another misnomer. What few parades the town had started at the high school where the marching band assembled. The parade grounds did boast a bandstand, where presidential candidates were rumored to have once spoken, the most recent of which, depending on who you talked to, was JFK, LBJ, or Richard Nixon, though there was no photographic evidence to support such claims.

The fairgrounds, parade grounds, or what-have-you boasted one annual function, hosting the Fourth of July picnic. Which was actually a pretty tough schedule for the meadow. If it rained on the Fourth of July, it washed out the whole year.

Not this year. The sky was cloudless, the day was sunny and bright, the temperature was in the mid-eighties. The turnout was tremendous. Aside from Chief Harper, everyone was there.

Cora could hardly get a parking place. The lot was full, and cars lined the service road. She finally wound up parking in front of the library and walking. As she trudged the half mile to the fairgrounds, it occurred to her she should have let Dan Finley drive her in.

It was a mob scene. Almost every inch of the meadow was taken up with people picnicking. Cora spotted Sherry and Jennifer on a blanket. Or at least Sherry on a blanket. Jennifer was running around and leaping over people. Such behavior might have seemed outrageous had not all the kids been doing it. Some were tossing Frisbees in the crowd. A few were actually playing football.

The high school marching band was assembled by the bandstand. It was, as far as Cora could remember, the closest the parade grounds had ever come to having a parade. Not that it was about to. Had the marching band actually marched, it would have trampled half the town.

Aaron Grant pushed his way through the crowd. "Hi, Cora. Thought you weren't going to make it."

"I was at the police station, bucking up the chief. He was freaking out about having to introduce Matt Greystone."

"You reassure him?"

"Not entirely. He bailed on the event to check out a robbery."

"Are you kidding me?"

"I think he was all right until Dan asked him if he'd rehearsed his remarks. I could see the panic setting in." Cora jerked her thumb in the direction of the Channel 8 van. "I see Rick Reed's all set to go. You get to park on your press pass?"

"The print media? We're lucky they let us in. I dropped off Sherry and Jennifer and parked in town."

Iris Cooper descended on them from the direction of the grandstand. The first selectman not only wore her Sunday best, but appeared to have applied an extra touch of makeup.

"Hi, Iris," Cora said. "Where's our golden boy?"

"Making a star's entrance, of course. He'll come driving up at one o'clock with the band playing and the cameras rolling. I'm supposed to meet the limo and give him the key to the city."

"We're hardly a city," Cora said.

"We don't have a key, either. It was just a figure of speech. Surely a puzzle constructor can get behind that."

Cora was sure a puzzle constructor could, she just didn't happen to be one.

"What's this I hear about Chief Harper?" Iris said.

"The chief is dealing with a police emergency."

"So I understand. I'd have told him how I felt about that except he didn't dare call me. He had Dan Finley do it. Anyway, Dan said you'd pinch-hit."

"You planning on peppering your welcome with baseball terms?"

Iris laughed. "I didn't even notice. Which

21

shows you how nervous I am. But you'll do it?"

"Do I get a signed baseball?"

A sudden excited buzz from the crowd attracted their attention.

Iris turned to look.

A black limousine was making its way through the crowd that had spilled out onto the road.

Iris sprang into action. "Clear the way! Cue the band! Volunteers, ready to direct the limo to the bandstand."

The limo rolled to a stop. The back door opened and a little man with a pencil-thin mustache and his hair slicked back stepped out. He wore a light-gray summer suit and a red tie knotted in a Windsor knot. He identified Iris Cooper's reception committee, walked over, and shook her hand.

Iris Cooper knew nothing about baseball, still she realized this was not the young pitcher she'd been waiting to welcome. "How do you do?" she said. "I'm Iris Cooper, first selectman."

Rick Reed, Channel 8's clueless on-camera reporter, was also aware this wasn't his quarry, but he wasn't about to miss the sound bite. He moved in behind Iris, thrust out the microphone to pick up the exchange.

"Pleased to meet you," the man said. "Lenny Schick, Matt's agent. You might want to knock off the music. Matt's not here."

"He's not coming?" Iris cried in dismay.

"Oh, he's coming. He wouldn't ride in the limo. That's Matt for you. He's walking from town, just like everybody else."

Per arrangement, Rick Reed's microphone was tied into the speakers on the bandstand, so the last exchange went out to the crowd. The surge of excited fans mobbed the road. Some even started down it back toward town.

"Oh, for goodness sakes," Iris said. She darted off to get her volunteers to control the crowd.

Rick Reed hesitated a moment, and followed.

"Looks like we're left in the lurch," Cora said. "Aren't you going to join the herd?"

"There are limits to how far I want to go for a puff piece," Aaron said. "Even one destined for the front page. You notice my wife and child resisted."

Over half the picnic blankets in the meadow were still occupied. Sherry was on hers. Jennifer, given more space, was racing in ever widening circles.

Watching the little girl, Cora's eye was

23

caught by a young couple at the far end of the meadow strolling hand in hand along the river.

Cora grinned. "Yeah, hang in here, Aaron."

Aaron looked. The couple had left the river and were weaving their way through the maze of picnic blankets.

The agent rushed to meet them. "There you are. It's about time. How am I supposed to run a campaign if you keep sabotaging it?"

The young man smiled good-naturedly, patted the little agent on the cheek. He was tall, clean-cut, with sandy hair and an engaging grin.

The woman on his arm was everything you'd expect a superstar's wife to be. Glossy auburn hair, girlish face, slim yet voluptuous body discreetly encased in loose-fitting cotton summer attire.

Matt Greystone had none of the steroidal bulk of the power pitcher who threw in the upper nineties. He was thin and wiry, a finesse pitcher, who mixed a fastball that was nothing to write home about with a slow curve and a slower changeup. Hitters waved at his pitches in frustration, wondering why they couldn't hit them.

Matt turned to Cora and Aaron. Before

he could introduce himself, his wife stepped in front of him. "Ditch the limo, Lenny."

"Jackie. How are you?"

"Fine. Ditch the limo."

"Jackie —"

"We walked here, Lenny. Let's not stage a photo op that makes it look like he came in a limo."

The agent gave in with poor grace, signaled to the limo driver to drive off.

Iris Cooper came surging back, with Rick Reed and his microphone in tow. "Matt Greystone. Iris Cooper. I'm the first selectman. It is an honor to welcome you to our town."

"Well, thank you, but that's not necessary. This is the Fourth of July. That's what the day is about. That's why all you people are here. I wouldn't want to do anything to take away from that."

"Well, that's a fine spirit, I'm sure," Iris Cooper said.

Perfectly handled, Cora thought. Now if only Iris is quick enough to forestall Rick Reed, who seemed poised with a question. In light of the young man's tasteful statement, it would be the worst of all possible worlds.

Wrong again.

Iris Cooper said, "There's just one person

I'd like you to meet. Allow me to introduce the Puzzle Lady, Cora Felton."

The young man looked pained as he turned to her. Cora felt for him. He couldn't rudely ignore her, but prolonging his time in the spotlight was the last thing in the world he wanted.

"And I would like to commend you on what you just said," Cora told him. "Today is the day to celebrate our country, not ourselves." She offered Matt her arm. "Would you allow me to walk you out of the spotlight?" Deliberately steering him away from Rick Reed, she proceeded to do so.

There was a stunned silence, followed by a rousing applause.

As they moved out of microphone range, Matt Greystone said to Cora in a low voice, "Thank you."

And just like that it was over. Iris Cooper looked startled. Rick Reed looked betrayed. Everyone clearly would have liked to see more of Matt Greystone. But in light of his modest comment about not wanting to undermine the Fourth of July, no one could resent him for it. Particularly since he hopped out among the blankets like an overgrown kid and joined the children throwing Frisbees. His good-natured enthusiasm was infectious. Cora couldn't help smiling.

Until she noticed he was throwing left-handed.

Cora felt a hand on her arm. She turned. Mrs. Matt Greystone was smiling at her.

"Cora. Hi. I'm Jackie. I just wanted to thank you."

Cora smiled, shook her hand. "For what?"

"Walking Matt out of there. This was all his agent's doing. He wants to keep Matt in the limelight. He's afraid Matt won't be the same when he comes back from his injury and he'll lose his market value."

"The Yankees still have to pay him."

"He's thinking of commercials, endorsements. He wants to make them now while Matt's still news."

"Won't a star player coming back from a serious injury be a huge news story?"

"If he's successful, sure. He's going to be out all year. He needs to come back next spring. But nothing's certain. If he does and goes ten and ten, good enough for your average starting pitcher, he'll look like he's completely lost it. And suppose he gets shelled. Suppose he gets sent down to the minor leagues. Comes back, can't cut it, gets sent down again."

"You're talking worst-case scenario," Cora

27

said. She gave Jackie an encouraging smile. "He looks like the type of guy who bounces back."

"Yeah. Anyway, I wanted to thank you. And I need your help."

"You got it," Cora said. "Moving here from New York is a big step. I know, I did it myself. So if there's anything I can do."

"Great," Jackie said. "I was hoping you could help me with this." She dug in her purse, came out with a sheet of paper, handed it to Cora.

It was a crossword puzzle.

UNTITLED

Across

1 "Just the facts, _____!"
5 Brussels-based alliance
9 Totally destroy
14 Jessica of "Dark Angel"
15 Like much folklore
16 Three-line verse
17 Start of a message
19 Conclude with
20 Parlor pieces
21 "Madame X" painter John Singer _____
23 _____ out (distribute)

25 Charlotte of "The Facts of Life"
26 Bowie's last stand
30 More of the message
35 Casaba and Crenshaw
37 Airline seat part
38 Fort _____, N.J.
39 Plugging away
40 Itsy-bitsy

42 Napoleon victory site of 1796
43 "_____ the season . . ."
44 Place for a cooling pie
45 T-shirt sizes
47 More of the message
50 Sports shocker
51 The whole shebang
52 Chuckwagon fare
54 Like canned nuts
58 Fill to excess
63 Goodie from Linz
64 End of the message
66 Hot to trot
67 Twistable treat
68 Without peer
69 Cattle zappers
70 Farmyard female
71 "Zounds!"

Down

1 Baseball's "Say Hey Kid"
2 Shaving gel additive
3 Touch on
4 Brewer's ingredient
5 Checking account come-on
6 Whitney Houston's longtime record label
7 Sunbather's goal
8 Car make until 2004, for short

9 Rehab treatment
10 Yellowstone employee
11 Intern, e.g.
12 Onion cover
13 Seek prey
18 Polish scent
22 Orderly groupings
24 Parsons of "Bonnie and Clyde"
26 Treasured violin
27 Allow to enter
28 Elite invitees
29 Witty rejoinder
31 Starbucks vessel
32 Ones on pedestals
33 Move like a crab
34 Live and breathe
36 Stop, as a yawn
41 One of the Mannings
42 400-meter path, perhaps
44 Some eBay users
46 "Is that an order?"
48 Put the kibosh on
49 Parade time
53 Truckee River feeder
54 Part of a flight
55 Winter coating
56 "In which case . . ."
57 Dire prophecy
59 Skye, for one
60 Bug-eyed

61 Ahi, e.g.
62 Gave the once-over
65 Address for a monk

CHAPTER 4

Cora's face fell.

The day had begun on such a positive note. She was going to meet Matt Greystone, one of her Yankee heroes. He had turned out to be a nice guy. She had ingratiated herself with him and his wife.

And now this.

A crossword puzzle. A rotten, stinking crossword puzzle. The worst of all possible worlds. A crossword puzzle she could not solve in a million years. And here was Matt Greystone's attractive young wife waiting for her to solve it, which she had about as much chance of doing as Matt had of pitching a perfect game on his broken arm.

"Where'd you get this?" Cora said.

"It came in the mail."

"To you?"

"No, to Matt."

"Who sent it?"

"I have no idea."

"What's Matt say about it?"

"Nothing. He has no idea who sent it."

"Does he do crossword puzzles?"

"No, he doesn't. He does Sudoku now and then. You know how it is with a starting pitcher. One day on, four days off. When he's sitting around, he'll sometimes do the Sudoku in the *Post*. But crosswords just aren't his thing."

"Do you do crosswords?"

"No, or I'd have solved it. That's why I was hoping you would."

"Why do you care?"

"Someone sent this to Matt with no explanation whatsoever. It's kind of strange. I thought the puzzle itself might tell me why." Jackie smiled. "Look, I know it's like walking up to a doctor at a party and telling him your symptoms. If you don't want to do it, I understand."

Cora smiled. "Hey, you want it solved, I'll take it home, see what it says. How can I get in touch with you?"

"Give me your cell phone. I'll program my number into it."

"I haven't got a cell phone."

"You haven't got a cell phone?"

"I never got out of the dark ages. You got a pen, you can write it on the back of the crossword puzzle."

Jackie scrawled her number on the cross-word puzzle, handed it over. "There's one other thing I was hoping you could help me with."

"What's that?"

Jackie pointed to the top of the puzzle. "See? It says 'Untitled.' What does that mean?"

"It means it doesn't have a title."

"Well, lots of puzzles don't have titles, don't they? Why say so?"

"I have no idea."

"Neither do I. But it's a little creepy. I mean, why would someone send that to Matt and say it was untitled?"

"Why indeed?" Cora said.

CHAPTER 5

Sherry Carter shook her head. "I can't leave you alone for a minute without you bringing back a crossword puzzle?"

"Believe me, it wasn't my idea."

"It's never your idea. You think that makes it any better?"

"What are you crabbing about? If it weren't for me, *you'd* be the Puzzle Lady and people would be bringing them directly to you."

"Not so often," Sherry said. "They expect you to solve the puzzle and the problem. I could solve the puzzle, which wouldn't help them much. It's the secret behind the puzzle they really want to know, and that's what you're good at."

"Yeah, well, I can't find the secret behind the puzzle unless you solve the damn thing. Besides, this one's different."

"How is it different?"

"This one has a title."

"Lots of puzzles have titles."

"Yeah, but it's 'Untitled.' "

"Huh? I thought you said it *has* a title."

"Yeah, it's 'Untitled.' "

"Cora —"

"Look."

Cora held up the puzzle.

Sherry took it, looked it over. "Oh, sure. This was created in Crossword Compiler. No one entered a title, so it says 'Untitled.' "

"Yeah, but —"

"But what?"

"I've seen lots of printouts of puzzles. They don't say 'Untitled.' They just don't have a title."

"Sure. Because that's what the constructor told Crossword Compiler. If you don't want it to have a title, you tell it not to have a title, and it leaves off the title. If you want a title, you type in a title and it prints. If you have it set for a title, but you don't enter one, it just says 'Untitled.' That's a puzzle you might want to have a title for, but you haven't titled it yet."

"So this was done deliberately?"

"Or as an oversight."

"Sherry —"

"When I solve this, maybe I can tell if the title was intended."

"So solve it."

"I would, but I'm busy."

"Doing what?"

"Your job. The Puzzle Lady column doesn't write itself. I gotta write a new one every day."

"Come on, Sherry. You're so good at it you can do it in your sleep. Solve it before I run into Matt Greystone's wife and she wants to know why I haven't."

"Don't worry, I'll get to it," Sherry said.

The phone rang. "Saved by the bell," Sherry said. She scooped it up. "Hi, Chief. Yeah, she's here."

Cora gave her a dirty look and picked up the phone. "Hi, Chief. It's all right. No one missed you."

"What?"

"In fact no one noticed you weren't there."

"That's what Dan said. He wasn't trying to get my goat?"

"No more than I am."

Cora filled Chief Harper in on the happenings at the fairgrounds.

"So it won't even make the evening news?" Harper said.

"Oh, I'm sure it will. But Rick Reed's going to have to make it up himself."

"Like what?"

"Oh, you know. Like 'Chief Harper ducked out on Matt Greystone, cutting short the introductions at the Bakerhaven fairgrounds. The premier Yankee pitcher did his best to carry on in the chief's absence, and left the stage after a curt dismissal of the entire proceedings.' "

"Oh, yeah? Well, the robbery turned out to be something."

"What was that?"

"It's a little complicated. You want to come down to the station?"

"Oh, great, Chief. First I fill in for you at the picnic, now you want me to solve your robbery."

"I don't want any such thing. I just want to talk it over with you to make sure I'm not going mad."

"Don't lob 'em across the plate like that, Chief."

"Very funny. Will you come in?"

"Not unless you give me a hint what this is all about."

"I told you. A robbery."

"And where was this robbery?"

"At Amanda Hoyt's."

"And just what was taken?"

"That's the thing. It may not have been taken. It may just be lost."

"All right. What has Amanda Hoyt lost?"

"Her memory."

CHAPTER 6

Cora drove down to the Bakerhaven police station. The town had emptied out in the late afternoon. It would fill up again when people came back to the fairgrounds to watch the fireworks. Though not nearly as many as for the picnic. The fireworks on the river could be seen from a good distance.

Cora parked in front of Cushman's Bake Shop. She couldn't resist going in for a corn muffin. Mrs. Cushman got her baked goods from the Silver Moon Bakery in Manhattan, so her pastries were top of the line. Cora ordered a corn muffin and a cappuccino, took it down to the police station.

Dan Finley was manning the desk.

"Did you tease the chief about Matt Greystone?" Cora said.

"Did you?"

"That's not the point. I'm not one of his officers."

"Come on, Cora. If I can't tease the chief

now and then, what's the use of the job?"

"Wasn't there something about protect and defend?"

"I didn't read the rules all that closely."

"Is the chief in?"

"That he is. Fourth of July, we got two policemen in the station. How do you like that?"

"How do *you* like that?"

"I get holiday pay. What's not to like?"

Cora went into the office, found the chief on the computer. That couldn't be good. The chief understood computers even less than Cora did when she started using them. Now she could whip around the Internet, going in and out of chat rooms, purchasing things online. Chief Harper needed help just logging on.

"What are you up to, Chief?"

"Just looking for help with my robbery."

"It is a robbery?"

"I think so."

"You're not sure?"

"She's not sure."

"Amanda Hoyt?"

"Yeah."

Amanda Hoyt was the village witch, at least as far as the kids were concerned. She was a medium, specialized in tarot cards and palm reading. She was rumored to hold séances, though no one would admit having been to one.

"And she's lost her memory?"

"Unless it was taken."

Cora blinked. "Please tell me you didn't say that, Chief."

"That was *my* first reaction. But apparently she has her data from her laptop backed up on some memory card."

"Oh, for goodness sakes."

"What?"

"She lost the memory card from her laptop?"

"Isn't that what I just said?"

"It's slightly less occult than what you just said."

"Huh?"

"If someone stole a memory card, it's a simple, straightforward crime."

"Except the thing's so damn small, she can't swear it's not lost."

"It's probably lost."

"Then why did someone break in?"

"Someone broke in?"

"Didn't I say that?"

"No, Chief. It's probably good you didn't introduce Matt Greystone if you can't even describe a simple crime."

"Sorry. This case has me spooked."

Cora's eyes widened. "You're afraid of the witch."

"I'm not afraid of the witch. There's just something creepy about it. Makes it hard to take what she says seriously."

"What's on this card that's so all-fired important?"

Harper made a face. "That's just it. She won't say."

"You're kidding."

"She says she can't violate a client's confidentiality. Just like if she was a doctor or lawyer or something."

"She has her séances on tape?"

"I don't know if it's recordings or written documents or what. Says she won't say, but it's confidential and she wants it back."

"If it's gone."

"She's sure it was taken."

"Why?"

"Because nothing else was."

"What makes her think *anything* was taken?"

"Because her house was broken into."

"How'd the intruder break in?"

"That's the thing."

Cora looked at him. "Everything about this case seems to be the thing. It has more qualifiers than a used-car warranty. What's the thing about this break-in?"

"I can't even be sure there was one."

"Excuse me?"

"According to Amanda the kitchen door was ajar. She swears she always keeps it locked. She claims the lock was forced."

"Was it?"

"It's an old house. There's scratches all over the door and the jamb."

"Are they fresh?"

"I can't tell. But enough of the wood's eaten away it wouldn't be hard to stick a knife blade between the door and the jamb if you wanted to slip the lock. So taking the woman at her word, her house was broken into."

"Say her house was broken into. She didn't have any money or jewelry worth taking?"

"She says nothing else is missing."

"It doesn't sound very promising, Chief. Frankly, I don't know what to suggest."

"I was hoping for a little more help than that."

"I'm not clear what you want me to do, Chief."

"I thought you might want to investigate the scene of the crime."

Cora cocked her head. "Oh, did you now?"

"Cora —"

44

"Investigate the scene of the crime. The scene of what crime? You're not even sure there is a crime. From what you tell me, there's nothing to see. So. You want me to talk to the witch."

"I just thought —"

"You're scared of the witch, so you want me to go talk to her."

"I'd like to know what her game is."

"You and half the town, Chief. You think she might tell me something she wouldn't tell you?"

"Why don't you run over there, say I sent you? At least it will show we're taking this thing seriously."

"It's the Fourth of July. She may not be home."

"She's home. I had Dan do a drive-by."

"He didn't mention that."

"I told him to keep it quiet."

"I can see why."

Before Chief Harper could retort, Cora was out the door.

CHAPTER 7

Cora had never been to Amanda Hoyt's house before. She'd seen it of course, but, like the rest of the town, she'd given it a wide berth. Trick-or-treaters skipped the house, and, even in the short time she had lived in town, there were tales, probably apocryphal, of unwise boys and girls who'd dared. Cora had kept away, not through any fear of the supernatural, but from a disinclination to disturb anyone who didn't wish to be disturbed.

If the woman had lost her memory, that was something else. It was a mystery, and Cora loved a mystery, despite her ritual feigned indifference with Chief Harper. It seemed only prudent to gripe about something besides crossword puzzles.

Not that there was anything strange about the house itself. It was, like most of the houses in Bakerhaven, a wood-frame house, white with green shutters, with two steps up to a wooden front porch. What kept people away was the woman's reputation.

Cora went up on the front steps and knocked.

The door was opened by the woman herself. She certainly didn't look like a witch. In a short skirt and light blue top over a body that could only be described as voluptuous, Amanda looked more like a call girl. At least, that was Cora's impression. Granted, she tended to judge her female competition harshly.

If Amanda Hoyt was equally catty she didn't show it. Her smile was welcoming. "Ah. Cora Felton. Come in. I've been expecting you."

"Really?" Cora said. "You saw it in your crystal ball, did you?"

The witch didn't take offense. She smiled at the witticism. "You often help Chief Harper out when he's faced with something he doesn't understand. It doesn't take a psychic to know he's out of his depth on this one. Do you know anything about computers?"

"I know more than Chief Harper."

"You would have to. He looked at mine as if it were a foreign object."

"Still he got the gist. Apparently you mislaid a memory card."

"It was stolen."

47

"Those cards are small. It's easy to lay a piece of paper over them."

"That didn't happen in this case. Someone broke in my kitchen door, came into my office, took the card out of the machine."

"It was left in the machine?"

"Absolutely."

"It's almost a reflex action when you've finished backing up the data to unplug the card."

"Not for me. I leave the card plugged in so it won't get lost."

Cora went in the kitchen and inspected the back door. It was as Chief Harper had described.

"This door was locked?"

"That's right."

"A burglar picked the lock and got in?"

"I'm afraid so."

"Has your house been broken into before?"

"Not that I know of. Of course, I haven't lived here that long."

"How long have you lived here?"

"I moved in two years ago. After my husband died."

"I didn't know that."

She smiled. "Why should you? I lived in New York. After Bill died, I didn't want to be in the apartment anymore."

"I can understand that."

"Yes. You've been married, haven't you?"

"Yes. Several times."

"And some of your husbands are dead."

"I didn't do it."

"I know."

"ESP?"

She shook her head. "I'm just a good judge of character."

"And that's all it is, isn't it?" Cora said. "This whole medium shtick. You size people up, tell them what they want to hear."

She smiled again. "I wish it were that simple. You quit drinking. Can I get you some tea?"

"I quit long before you came to town."

"I know."

"Do you do that deliberately?"

"What?"

"Try to piss me off."

"Not at all. So, tea? No, you hate tea. Everyone's always offering you tea. Iced tea would be better, but not great. Let's see. Ah! Iced cappuccino. Here you go. I've got an espresso machine. I put the milk in this little thermos, put it on the spindle, press the button, and a light comes on and it froths the milk. Press it and hold it, and the light turns blue and it froths the milk without heating it up."

Amanda made the iced cappuccinos. Cora tasted one. They weren't Frappuccinos, but they weren't half-bad.

"I don't have the ice crushing machine," Amanda said.

"What?"

"To make a Frappuccino. That's what you'd prefer. So would I, but I make do with these. So, let's go back in the living room, sit down, and tell me what's on your mind."

"This is not a session," Cora said as they sat down.

"Of course not. I meant with regard to my case. Chief Harper has essentially assigned it to you, hasn't he? Not that I mind. You've had great success."

Cora settled back in her chair, sipped her iced cappuccino. "Before we go any further, I have one question."

"What's that?"

"There's no crossword puzzle involved, is there?"

Amanda frowned. "Crossword puzzle?"

"When the chief assigns me something, often it's because there's a crossword puzzle involved. He thinks it's my field of expertise so I should handle it."

"Not this time."

"I'm glad to hear it. Then, conceding the fact something was stolen, we have a simple, straightforward robbery. So, let's discuss your case. You had a memory card stolen. A memory card is merely for backing up files that are on your computer. The card is gone, but the original files still exist."

"Unless the person who stole them deleted some of the files."

"Is there any evidence that happened?"

"Nothing that jumps out at me. Obviously I haven't gone through everything."

"Until we discover otherwise, let's assume the files still exist. I'm assuming you also print out hard copies in case a power surge wipes out everything."

"I have surge protectors."

"So do I. I still print anything important. From the size of the file cabinets in the corner I would say you do, too."

"Yes, I do."

"The file cabinets are kept locked?"

"They are."

"Any indication they were broken into?"

"No."

"What sort of files do you keep in there?"

"I'm sorry, that's confidential."

Cora rolled her eyes.

Amanda smiled. "You think this is all witchcraft, don't you?"

Cora coughed. Having accused the chief of being afraid of the witch, she was hard-pressed to deny it. Still, Cora had not survived a half-dozen odd husbands plus a bogus profession without having mastered some of the fine arts of prevarication. "I think you do things I don't understand. And I'm not sure any explanation would help me."

"Well put. I try to figure out what people need, and help them get it. My methods of help are as varied as people's needs."

"You're a licensed therapist?"

She smiled. "A psychiatrist, actually. But people don't think of me that way. There is no degree for what I practice. I am, however, rather good at it. I don't advertise, my clients come by word of mouth, and my word of mouth is good."

"Who would you give as a reference?"

"I wouldn't. People who contact me already have a reference, the person who sent them. If that isn't sufficient, they're free to seek help elsewhere."

"What kind of help do you offer?"

"Are you looking for help?"

"No, I'm looking for your memory card."

She smiled again. "Well put. I'm afraid the usual lines of inquiry aren't going to help you much. You might as well abandon them. Assume the memory card is a price-less antique, for instance a diamond-studded tiara once worn by Queen Victoria."

"Did she allow herself such excess?"

"Let's say she did. And let's say I had it, and let's say someone stole it. Just assume the memory card is a valuable piece of property, and proceed accordingly."

"That's not going to work," Cora said, "and I can't imagine you wouldn't know why. In the case of your diamond-studded tiara there are limited avenues for disposing of such property."

"I would imagine there were limited avenues for disposing of a memory card, too."

"Yes, but the police don't know what they are. And they're not going to find out if you won't tell them what's on the memory card."

The witch nodded. "It's a puzzle, isn't it?" She smiled. "No wonder they sent you."

CHAPTER 8

"It's a robbery, Chief."

Chief Harper had been packing up his desk to go home. He looked up and frowned. "What?"

"She was robbed. Someone broke in and stole her memory card."

"Oh, my God," Harper said. "You've gone over to the dark side." He got up from his desk, walked out of his office. "Did you hear that, Dan? She's in league with the witch."

"Yeah, she told me," Dan said.

"What did you tell her?"

"I told her to tell you."

"Dan —"

Dan Finley put up his hands. "You sent her out there. You think I'm going to dismiss the report you asked her to get?"

"And I'm certainly grateful," Harper said. "Though I didn't expect to have a report so soon."

"I believe in giving service," Cora said.

"So, here's your report. The woman is not a witch, she's a licensed therapist. She's not scatterbrained. She's precise and methodical. If she says the card was plugged into her computer, it was plugged into her computer."

"What was on the card?"

"She won't say."

"See, this is where it breaks down for me. I try to be broadminded, but the minute you make me play guessing games about what was stolen, I lose interest. It kind of curtails any speculation as to who the perpetrator might be."

"Oh, so that's how you solve crimes, Chief. By speculation. Surely more effective than investigation and analysis. I can see why this one wouldn't interest you."

Dan Finley suppressed a giggle.

"Don't encourage her," Chief Harper said. "You think this case deserves investigation?"

"Why not? It's not like there's some crime wave you're dealing with."

Chief Harper frowned. He cocked his head, looked at Cora quizzically. "You like her. I can't imagine that. Why would you like her? This is the type of woman you would normally think of as competition."

"Why, Chief. I had no idea you were such an astute judge of women."

Harper flushed. "Sorry. I just can't see you embracing a woman with such a dubious profession. Particularly when your own expertise is so grounded in fact."

"I'd quit, Chief," Dan said. "You're just digging the hole deeper."

"What's wrong with that?" Harper said.

"I don't know, but I'm sure Cora will tell us."

Harper caught the twinkle in his eye. "All right. You two are making fun of me. I'd like to close up the station in time for the fireworks. If I'm late taking my wife, there'll be hell to pay."

"A rather sad assessment of the authority of our mighty chief of police," Dan Finley observed.

"You've obviously never been married, Dan," Cora said, "or you'd recognize a simple universal truth."

CHAPTER 9

Cora, Sherry, Aaron, and Jennifer watched the fireworks from the fairgrounds. It was a first for Cora. For years Cora had ignored the fireworks from the comfort of her own home. But that was before her niece had a child old enough to be interested. If Jennifer liked it, it was entertainment. Not the activity itself, but the activity of watching her enjoy the activity.

The fairgrounds were only half-full, which was par for the course. Half the townspeople lived close enough to see it from their own backyards. Others ignored it completely. After all, it happened every year, and unlike the impressive displays on the Hudson, it was really nothing to write home about.

Chief Harper lived close enough to town that he could have seen it from his backyard, but that would not have satisfied his wife, who saw it as an opportunity to socialize. The Harpers were there in full force. Even their daughter, Clara, was home for the holiday, though Cora would not have recognized the poised young lady whom she had first met as a teenaged schoolgirl. It, like so many things these days, gave her pause. Cora always found it amazing how people around her aged while she stayed remarkably young.

Matt Greystone was not among those present. Cora could attest to the fact, as could most of the rest of the town. There was more craning of the necks than usual, and not in the direction of the sky.

"See," Sherry said to Cora. "He's not even here."

"Who?"

"Matt Greystone. I told you he wouldn't be."

Sherry hadn't gotten around to solving the crossword puzzle yet. Cora had been afraid she'd run into Matt Greystone's wife and not be prepared.

"I wasn't looking for him," Cora said.

"Oh? Who were you looking for?"

"The witch. And guess what? She's right over there."

Amanda Hoyt was indeed standing with two other women. From their body language, they were not close friends.

"Which makes this a rare opportunity,"

Cora said.

"What do you mean?"

"I can't think of another time when I can count on her being anywhere."

"So?"

"So I'd be a damn fool not to take advantage of it."

Sherry's eyes widened. "Cora!"

"What?"

"You're going to break into the house to solve the robbery?"

"It does seem a little counterintuitive."

"Counterintuitive? Is that your word for the day?"

" 'Bite me' is my word for the day."

"That's two words."

"They're the nicest two I can think of. After you ruined my Fourth of July by not solving the crossword puzzle."

"Ruined your Fourth of July? You never celebrate the Fourth of July. You couldn't care less about the Fourth of July. Don't change the subject. You're going to break into a house. As if that weren't bad enough, you just made me an accessory before and after the fact by telling me about it."

"Sorry about that. I was hoping you'd keep an eye on her so she wouldn't come home and catch me in the act."

"I don't know the woman. What do you

expect me to do, run up and tackle her?"

"No, but I'd appreciate a heads-up."

"What do you want me to do, call you on the cell phone you don't have? Or do you want me to loan you mine, so when you're caught they'll have evidence I was complicit?"

"No. Just call *her* phone."

"What?"

"When I talked to her I got her phone number." Cora handed Sherry a piece of paper. "Here you go. If she starts to leave, call this number, let it ring twice, and hang up. When I hear that I'll get the hell out."

Sherry looked at the paper. "You had this ready the whole time."

"So?"

"You planned this. You just didn't tell me, because you knew I wouldn't do it."

"You're not going to do it? That's okay. I understand. You can visit me in jail."

Cora smiled at her niece and was gone before Sherry could stop her.

CHAPTER 10

The witch's door was locked. That was unfortunate. At least half of the residents of Bakerhaven left their houses unlocked. Of course, most of them had never been robbed. A woman whose house had been burglarized could be excused for being a tad cautious.

The front door lock appeared substantial. Cora was a woman of many talents, but picking locks was not among them. She acknowledged it as a flaw in her education.

The kitchen door, she recollected, was not nearly as formidable. It had also been recently broken into. Some of the wood around the lock was actually missing. It occurred to Cora a good credit card would probably jimmy it. It occurred to her a bad credit card would probably break off and be stuck in there with her name on it.

Cora fished in her floppy drawstring purse. The first thing she encountered was a Smith & Wesson revolver, but she wasn't about to shoot the lock off. She pawed further, and finally found her Swiss army knife, offering a wide selection of blades. She opted for the screwdriver, which proved to be too short for the purpose. The awl was also short. The large blade was perfect, but she hated to dull it. She stuck it in the door, pushed down, and the lock clicked back.

The kitchen was dark, but there was a light on in the living room, not an uncommon practice among people hoping to discourage robbers, or not wanting to stub their toes in the dark. Cora left the kitchen light out, made her way down the hallway by the light from the living room. In the study, she risked the light. She figured the odds of a neighbor seeing it go on, knowing the witch wasn't at home, and putting two and two together were rather slim.

The computer was on. Cora first checked to see if there was a memory card, not that she intended to steal it. Still, the information on it would be the most likely source of why someone wanted to steal it before. But there was no card plugged into the machine.

Cora sat down at the desk chair, clicked the mouse, and the computer sprang to life.

Cora was immediately greeted by a number of helpful icons. They were not, however, helpfully titled. They were merely small designs offering hints as to what they might be.

Cora clicked on a tiger's head and came up with a program similar to Quicken. As far as Cora could tell, it differed from Quicken only in not being Quicken. She was unable to see how different, since it wouldn't open without a password. Cora tried a few generic passwords, such as "1234" and "password" to no avail. She wished she knew the name of the witch's latest pet.

Cora found an icon that was either Sigmund Freud or one of the Smith Brothers cough drop boys. She clicked on it and discovered the witch's client file. It also required a password. On a whim Cora tried "Sigmund," "Freud," and "Sigmund Freud." None worked. She wondered vaguely what the first names of the Smith Brothers were.

Cora gave up the computer as a lost cause. After all, the witch had files. Of course, they were locked. On inspection, the locks fell somewhere between the unpickable front door, and the pickable kitchen door.

Cora retrieved a paper clip from the desk drawer, and went to work on the locks.

CHAPTER 11

Aaron Grant joined his family at the fireworks.

"Ah," Sherry said. "You managed to tear yourself away from Becky Baldwin."

Aaron winced. Becky had been his high school sweetheart. There was nothing between them now, though Cora took great delight in implying that there was. The fact that Aaron was a reporter and the attractive young Ms. Baldwin was Bakerhaven's resident attorney meant they were often thrown together, much to Cora's amusement.

"I was just asking if she had a case."

"Does she?"

"No."

"Well, that couldn't have taken very long."

"Actually I was sounding her out on whether she might be able to line up some business from Matt Greystone."

"I would imagine he has a team of lawyers in his stable."

65

"That's what she said."

"Depressed, is she? Playing the poor little small-town-lawyer-can't-get-a-case card."

"You're the one who said Matt Greystone wouldn't hire her. Aside from that, she isn't interested."

"I know she isn't interested in married men."

"Now you sound like Cora."

"I do, don't I?"

"Where is Cora, by the way?"

"She stepped out for a while."

"Stepped out? We're at the fireworks."

"She had something to take care of."

"Something I can write about?"

"No."

"That figures. It's never something I can write about."

Sherry craned her neck.

"What are you doing?" Aaron said.

"What do you mean?"

"You're looking over my shoulder. What are you looking at?"

"Ah, hell."

"Are you doing something wrong?"

"Are you going to turn me in? Or, worse, write about me?"

"What's Cora done now?"

"Why do you always think it's Cora?"

"Because it always is. Plus, she's gone, and

66

you won't tell me why."

"I didn't say I wouldn't tell you why, I said you couldn't write it."

"All right, why?"

"Cora wanted me to warn her if the witch went home."

"Nice alliteration. Wanna translate that for me?"

"There's nothing to translate. That's the truth, the whole truth, and nothing but the truth."

"And how are you supposed to warn her?"

"Oh."

"Sherry —"

"Aaron, sweetie, would you mind not standing in my sightline of the witch?"

"Relax. She's not going to leave until the fireworks are over."

"Oh, hell."

"What?"

"She's leaving."

"Really?"

"You and your big mouth."

"Hey, it's not like I made her leave."

"It's *exactly* like you made her leave." Sherry tugged her cell phone out of her pocket. "Damn it, where's the number?"

"What number?"

"Shhh!" Sherry tugged the paper out of her pocket. She held it up, punched the number into her cell phone.

Across the lawn, Amanda Hoyt was almost to her car. She stopped, dug in her purse, fished out her cell phone.

Sherry switched off her phone on the second ring.

Amanda looked at her phone, shrugged, and slipped it back in her purse.

Sherry lowered her phone. "Oops."

CHAPTER 12

Cora couldn't get the file cabinet open, and it wasn't for lack of trying. She'd exhausted the paper clip, moved on to her nail file, even tried an old mailbox key from her apartment in the City. In frustration, she whipped out the screwdriver blade from the Swiss army knife. Ignoring the keyhole, she stuck it right under the lip of the file itself, and pried hard.

With a rending of metal the drawer popped open. The bar from the lock was still extended, but Cora had managed to bend the slot it went into. It did not look good. The witch would know someone had been there.

Well, the deed was done. The drawer was open. She might as well take a look.

The file drawer Cora had pried open was labeled "G–M." Cora jerked it open.

The name Greystone leapt out at her.

Before Cora had time to take it in, a siren

split the air. The witch had her files alarmed!

Cora slammed the drawer, hoping the alarm would stop. It didn't. If it was sounding there, it was probably sounding in the police station. Cora prayed it wasn't. Still, she was bound and determined to get the hell out of there. The same neighbors who wouldn't notice a light going on in the study might be less apt to miss an air-raid siren.

Cora sprinted for the kitchen, wrenched open the door.

Headlights were turning into the driveway.

Cora hopped over the rail at the back of the porch. She landed in a heap, clambered to her feet, and ran around the back of the house.

The damn woman had a fence. It wasn't that high, but Cora had thought her fence-climbing days were behind her. She had long resolved never again to put herself in the position of jumping out the bedroom window when some man's wife came home unexpectedly.

On the other hand, a lifetime of having done so stood her in good stead. Cora clawed her way up the fence, balanced on the top for a moment, and rolled over into the next yard.

A car door slammed.

The witch or the police? Cora wasn't looking forward to seeing either one.

Lights snapped on at the house next door. The witch's neighbor had floodlights on his garage, but they were aimed toward the street. Surely they wouldn't illuminate an intruder in the backyard.

A man's voice yelled over the sound of the alarm, "Amanda, what the hell did you do?"

"What did I do? I just got here. You think I set off the alarm?"

"Well, can you shut the damn thing off?"

Cora could imagine the witch's teeth grinding together in helpless frustration. Not that she was waiting around to hear the end of the argument. The witch was home, the cops were on the way. The intervention of the neighbor was the diversion she needed to get to her car.

Cora scurried through the bushes around the back of the neighbor's house, slipped into the next neighbor's backyard, and worked her way around the far side of their house. If they were home, their attention would be focused in the other direction.

Cora reached her car, slipped in, and started the engine. As she drove slowly down the road with her lights out, she could hear the siren of the police car arriving from the other direction.

CHAPTER 13

Cora got home to find Sherry in the kitchen brewing a cup of coffee.

"You're home early," Cora said.

"The fireworks display was unspectacular," Sherry said. "Even Jennifer got bored."

"Oh, is that right?"

Sherry smiled. "So how was your day?"

"How was my day? What happened with the heads-up?"

"What happened with the heads-up is you don't have a cell phone."

"You were supposed to call me on *her* phone."

"Yes, but you don't have a cell phone, so it never occurs to you other people do. So when you asked for her number, she didn't give you her home number, she gave you her cell phone. She answered it just before she drove off, but I couldn't think of anything I wanted to say to her so I hung up. So she came home and surprised you?"

"Actually the alarm on the file cabinet

surprised me. She was just the icing on the cake."

"But you got away?"

"I did, and I need your help."

"Why? You figure I didn't actually warn you, so I owe you?"

"No, but I got another kick in the head aside from the file cabinet being alarmed. One of the files happens to be labeled 'Greystone.' "

"Uh oh. What's in it?"

"I don't know. The alarm went off and the witch came home. It seemed like a good time to leave."

"She didn't see you?"

"No."

"Are you sure?"

"If she had, the police would be here by now."

"So you're in the clear. A normal person would thank their lucky stars and butt the hell out."

"Yeah, but I got something else hanging over my head."

"What's that?"

"The crossword puzzle. I don't know what's in the Greystone file, but I've got a crossword puzzle connected to the Greystones that just might shed some light on the situation."

"How could it possibly do that?"

"What if the message is 'Check the hard files'?"

"Yeah, well it won't be."

"How do you know?"

Sherry sighed. "All right, I'll take a look at it. You want a cup of coffee?"

"Coffee doesn't keep you up?"

"I have a preschooler. Nothing keeps me up."

"Sure, let's have coffee."

"Cream and sugar?"

"Shoot the works."

Sherry poured two mugs of coffee. She slid a quart of milk and a bowl of sugar across the kitchen table. "You know where the spoons are?"

"It's my kitchen."

"Learned to boil water yet?"

Sherry was out the door before Cora could come up with an activity to inquire whether she had learned to do yet. She was back in minutes with the crossword puzzle.

"You stopped to solve it?" Cora said.

"It was upstairs. I looked in on Jennifer."

"She's still awake?"

"I think I gave her too much coffee."

Cora cocked her head. "It occurs to me you always seem to have too much fun when I'm in trouble."

"Has it ever occurred to you you're always in trouble?"

"Constantly. You wanna solve that puzzle, or you just gonna stand there sniping at me?"

"It's a tough decision," Sherry said. She sat down at the table, took a sip of coffee, picked up a pencil, and attacked the puzzle.

Cora watched in amazement. "I can't even *read* the clues that fast," she said.

Sherry ignored her, continued working on the puzzle.

"Are you just filling in random letters?"

"You're not helping," Sherry said without breaking stride.

"You don't look like you need help."

"You're going to need help in a minute. 'Puzzle Lady impaled by pencil. Discovered with crossword puzzle stuffed in mouth.' "

Sherry set down the pencil.

"I'm impressed," Cora said. "You never missed a beat. Even while yammering at me."

"Oh, *I* was yammering at *you*?" Sherry said.

"Incessantly. I can forgive you, though, because you were working on a puzzle."

Sherry's mouth dropped open.

"What?"

"YOU'LL FIND
A SURPRISE
IN THE FILE
OF THIS GUY."

"Are you kidding me?"

"No."

"Did you just make that up?"

"Of course not."

"Give me a break. I said something about the files and you're putting me on."

Sherry held out the puzzle. "See for yourself."

```
 M  A  A  M  ▐  N  A  T  O  ▐  T  R  A  S  H
 A  L  B  A  ▐  O  R  A  L  ▐  H  A  I  K  U
 Y  O  U  L  L  F  I  N  D  ▐  E  N  D  I  N
 S  E  T  T  E  E  S  ▐  S  A  R  G  E  N  T
 ▐  ▐  M  E  T  E  ▐  R  A  E  ▐  ▐
 A  L  A  M  O  ▐  A  S  U  R  P  R  I  S  E
 M  E  L  O  N  S  ▐  T  R  A  Y  ▐  D  I  X
 A  T  I  T  ▐  T  E  E  N  Y  ▐  L  O  D  I
 T  I  S  ▐  S  I  L  L  ▐  S  M  A  L  L  S
 I  N  T  H  E  F  I  L  E  ▐  U  P  S  E  T
 ▐  A  L  L  ▐  E  A  T  S  ▐  ▐
 S  H  E  L  L  E  D  ▐  S  A  T  I  A  T  E
 T  O  R  T  E  ▐  O  F  T  H  I  S  G  U  Y
 E  A  G  E  R  ▐  O  R  E  O  ▐  L  O  N  E
 P  R  O  D  S  ▐  M  A  R  E  ▐  E  G  A  D
```

Cora pointed to the puzzle.

"I have no doubt you wrote it there. I said you were filling in letters without looking at the clues. That's what you did. Copied in your stupid little poem just to pay me back for making you solve the damn thing. You've had your laugh. Now what does it really say?"

"Now who's putting who on?" Sherry said. "You solved a copy of this before you gave it to me, didn't you? So you could predict what it was going to say and blow my mind."

"You're too young to say 'blow my mind.' It's a sixties expression."

"I know it's a sixties expression. I make up crossword puzzles. You solved it, didn't you?"

"You know I can't."

"So you had Harvey Beerbaum solve it for you. That's how you knew what it said, and that's why you were so eager to get into the witch's files tonight."

Cora made a few remarks regarding the amount of credence she placed in Sherry's supposition. Even a casual observer would have deduced she didn't place much.

"You really didn't know what the puzzle said until just now?" Sherry said.

"It really says what you say it did?" Cora

countered.

"Yeah," Sherry said. "What do you think it means?"

"I'm in a lot of trouble."

Chapter 14

Chief Harper didn't look pleased. Cora hadn't expected he would. Still, he looked dramatically displeased. "Do you know where I was last night?"

Cora could take a guess. The sirens she had heard driving away from the witch's house were a fairly good clue. So was the fact Chief Harper had summoned her to the police station first thing next morning. She counted herself lucky she hadn't been summoned the night before.

"I saw you at the fireworks," Cora said.

"I saw you there, too. At least I saw you *before* the fireworks. I can't say I saw you *during* the fireworks, because I wasn't *there* during the fireworks, a fact my wife is not particularly happy with."

"You want me to talk to your wife?"

"No, I want you to take another guess as to where I was last night. *During* the fireworks. Wanna take a whack at that?"

"From your disposition I'd say you were probably investigating a crime."

"Good guess. Wanna take a guess which crime?"

"Is that a pun, Chief?"

"What?"

"Which crime? The crime involving the witch?"

"Yes, that's exactly the crime I was talking about. And what a coincidence you got it in one guess."

"Well, don't give me too much credit, that's the only crime you have at the moment."

"No, it isn't. I happen to have *two* crimes at the moment. They both happen to be robberies at the witch's house, but they happen to be two separate crimes."

"What did they take this time?"

"I don't know."

"That doesn't sound like a very fruitful investigation, Chief. No wonder you called me in."

"I called you in because you weren't at the fireworks last night."

"How do you know that if you weren't there yourself?"

"I was there. I got a call that an alarm had gone off at the witch's house. I figured you'd want to check it out with me, so I looked around and you weren't there."

"I promise I won't tell anyone else that you wasted time looking for me while the thief got away."

"Cora."

"Particularly Rick Reed. I won't tell Rick Reed. He would just twist a statement like that into something awful."

"Did you rob the witch's house last night?"

"Of course not. I'm a law-abiding citizen."

"So if I were to send Dan Finley to take fingerprints none of them would be yours?"

"Lots of them would be mine. I was just there yesterday afternoon. Anyway, I'm dying to hear about this robbery, Chief. What was taken this time? Oh, that's right. You don't know."

"No, I don't. Can I assume you do?"

"You can assume anything you like. That doesn't make it true. You said there was an alarm?"

"Yes. Didn't you hear it?"

"From the parade grounds? How loud was this alarm? And how come an alarm didn't go off the first time? Or did it?"

"No, it didn't. Anyway, the burglar broke into her files."

"On the computer?"

"No, her actual files. The doors weren't

alarmed. The file cabinet was."

"The file cabinet? I thought you said he didn't take anything."

"I didn't say he didn't take anything. And I didn't say it was a he. The drawer of the file cabinet was jimmied open. That set off the alarm."

"So this time he took an actual file?"

"Not necessarily. The intruder may have just *looked at* a file."

"Looked at a file?"

"Yes."

"Would that be considered burglary? Stealing knowledge?"

"I have no idea, and I'm not getting drawn into the argument. The point is the files may have been broken into just so someone could look through them without actually taking anything."

"Do you have any evidence to support that theory?"

"Actually, I do."

That caught Cora up short. "What?"

"I have a file folder from the drawer. Amanda Hoyt gave it to me to process for fingerprints to see if anyone had tampered with it."

"She gave you a file?"

"Not the file. Just the folder."

"The file had been stolen?"

82

"No, the file was there. She removed it from the folder."

"Ah. That's where you get the theory the file was looked at rather than stolen."

"That's right."

"Unless the thief was after something in particular."

"Huh?"

"Well, there could have been a document in the file the burglar wanted. He riffled through the file, found it, and took it. Then you'd have an actual burglary instead of an invasion of privacy."

"Invasion of privacy? Are you looking toward a potential plea bargain, Cora?"

"No, but I'm sure Becky Baldwin will be, if you ever manage to charge anybody with this crime. Becky will be shooting for a dismissal of charges, or at least an acquittal, but I'm sure she'll have thought of a plea bargain, too."

"Anyway, the file's being processed for prints." Chief Harper cocked his head. "You didn't happen to touch it by any chance, did you?"

"Luckily, when I inspected the crime scene, the file cabinet was locked. So, Chief, are you ready for the sixty-four-thousand-dollar question? Whose file folder was it?"

"Amanda Hoyt's."

"Don't be a doofus. What was the name on the file?"

"I don't know. She removed it before she gave it to me."

"I beg your pardon?"

"The file folders in her file cabinet have clear plastic tabs on the top. The kind you type the name of the file on a sheet of paper, cut it out, and slide it into the tab. She slid the paper out before she gave it to me."

"That's less than helpful."

"No kidding."

"Did you point that out to her?"

"I did, but she didn't care. Her clients' files were private. She was perfectly happy to give me the folder."

"What about the drawer itself? The one that was broken into?"

"What about it?"

"Wasn't the drawer labeled?"

"Yes, for all the good it does us. The file came from the drawer labeled 'G dash M.' "

"All right, that's something. Did you see her take the file out of the drawer?"

"Yes, but I couldn't see the name on it."

"Could you see what position it was in the file? In the front, in the middle, in the back?"

"It was near the front."

"Well, that's very interesting. And very

lucky for me."

"What do you mean?"

"Cora Felton. My last name begins with an 'F.' So the file that was taken couldn't be mine." She shook her head. "On the other hand, Chief, it could be yours. Harper? 'H'? About as close to the front as you can get."

"Uh huh," Chief Harper said. "Now what did you really think?"

"What do you mean?"

"When I said it was near the front of the file, you reacted. Then you blathered some nonsense about how it couldn't be your file but it could be mine. What were you really thinking?"

"Oh, the demon interrogator. Can't slip anything by you. You got me, Chief. I was thinking the name Greystone begins with a 'G.' Maybe you'll get to interview our new celebrity after all. Why don't you run him in?"

"Very funny. What were you really thinking?"

Cora grimaced. "I can't come up with a secret agenda, Chief. I'd really like to keep something from you, but I can't even make up anything suspicious. Let me ask you this: were the drawers just for patients' files? I mean, is it possible the file could be something else?"

"Like what?"

"Well, insurance starts with an 'I.' Or IRS forms."

"IRS forms?"

"Sure."

"You mean tax forms? Why wouldn't she label it 'TAXES' like everybody else?"

"I'm throwing out ideas, Chief. They can't all be winners. The important thing is the concept. Now you'll have it in mind. Later on, if something jumps out at you. Like you find out a drug cartel is operating out of Bakerhaven and you say, 'Aha, H is for Heroin.' "

"Sounds like a Sue Grafton title."

"You read Sue Grafton, Chief?"

"I've heard of the damn books." Harper looked at Cora narrowly. "You know, I was starting to think you had nothing to hide. But that's a lot of talk about nothing, even for you. You're sure there's nothing you're not telling me?"

Cora smiled, and patted him on the cheek. "Would I hold out on you, Chief?"

CHAPTER 15

Cora Felton came out of the police station, walked down the alley, and took the stairs up to Becky Baldwin's office. Becky lived over a pizza parlor, and the aromas had a tendency to seep up. The special of the day seemed to be sausage and peppers.

The attractive young attorney was sitting at her desk reading a paperback thriller.

"Really," Cora said. "Couldn't you even *look* busy? Suppose I was a client?"

"Then you'd either have a reason to hire me or not. My lack of a conflicting case would hardly be a deterrent."

Cora nodded approvingly. "Well argued. You must be good in court."

"I'm not going to speculate on what you must be good in. It wouldn't be fair since I've been your attorney."

"And might be again," Cora said.

"Oh?"

"I seem to be in need of an attorney. My

thoughts naturally turned to you."

"That might be more flattering if I weren't the only one in town. Do you really need an attorney, or are you just screwing around?"

"A little of both."

"Cora."

"Well, I haven't killed anyone. We're talking about some rather trivial crimes."

"Such as?"

"Breaking and entering, burglary, obstructing justice, withholding evidence, and conspiring to conceal a crime."

"You consider those trivial charges?"

"Well, compared to murder."

"Are you telling me you're guilty of those charges?"

"Of course not. I'm innocent. Just like all of your clients. I understand you couldn't help me if I were guilty. But since I'm innocent you'll do your best to save me from the clutches of the law."

"So what are you accused of doing?"

"Nothing. That's the beauty of it. No one has accused me of anything. Of course, if I'd been more forthcoming about the situation, Chief Harper might have thought differently."

Becky groaned. "What did you do now?" Before Cora could answer she put up her hand. "I mean what is it you are afraid some ill-informed minion of the law might be misguided enough to suspect you of having done?"

"Breaking into the witch's house."

"You swore up and down you didn't do it."

"I didn't. That is absolutely true. When her house was broken into I barely even knew where the woman lived."

"So, what's the problem?"

"Well, it seems her house was broken into again."

"Cora."

"It's not my fault. The problem with inspecting a crime scene is if you're not the police they won't let you do it."

"I thought Chief Harper *let* you inspect the crime scene."

"He did. As part of the police investigation. But the police had no right to look at the woman's confidential files."

"Are you saying you looked in her confidential files?"

"Absolutely not. I have never laid eyes on *anything* in the woman's confidential files. And anyone who says I did is a police officer being suckered in by the circumstantial and physical evidence to come to the totally unfair conclusion that I did."

"And what might lead the police to make

this unfounded supposition?"

"The physical evidence."

"See, this is where I want to strangle you. You've virtually told me you're guilty of a breaking and entering and you want me to cover it up."

"Not at all."

"Let's get at this another way. What is it the police think you did?"

"Chief Harper thinks I broke into the woman's house last night, jimmied a file drawer open, and looked through a particular file."

"What particular file?"

"He doesn't know. But the witch does. She pulled that file from the file cabinet, removed the label from the file folder, took the files out of it, and gave the folder to Chief Harper to fingerprint."

"So the witch expected a particular file to be targeted. Had you looked through that file?"

"No, and I'm safe to say that because I haven't looked through *any* files in that file cabinet."

"So you don't know which file that is?"

"Oh."

"Cora."

"Well, it's not my fault. The drawer is labeled G through M. The file she gave the chief was somewhere near the front."

"So?"

"If I knew the name on one of the files in the front, there's a chance it might be that."

"And how could you possibly know the name on one of the files in the front?"

"Would you like me to bore you with a hypothetical?"

"Not unless you bore me with a retainer. We're reaching the point where I may have to rely on attorney/client privilege."

Cora dug in her purse, fished out her wallet. She snapped it open, took out a dollar, and slapped it on the desk. "There. You're retained."

"At last I can pay the rent," Becky said dryly. "Hit me with your hypothetical."

"Suppose I happened to know one of the folders in that file drawer was labeled 'Greystone'?"

Becky's mouth fell open. "Our new celebrity? I would say your retainer is starting to look less than adequate."

"Yeah," Cora said. "If that's the case, we've got a mystery I can't solve with all kinds of ramifications."

"You think Harper will figure it out?"

"No."

"It won't occur to him Greystone starts with a 'G'?"

"I told him it does."

"You what?"

"I told him Greystone starts with a 'G' and maybe he'd get a chance to interview him after all. He thought I was making fun of him."

"Weren't you?"

"Yes, but not the way he thought. Now, you wanna hear the bad part?"

Becky raised her eyebrows. "The bad part? You mean that was the good part?"

"Well, it's not as bad as this."

"Really? I can't wait."

"Yesterday afternoon Matt Greystone's wife gave me a crossword puzzle she said was sent to her husband. She wanted me to solve it, not knowing I can't. The solution to that puzzle was 'You'll find a surprise in the files of this guy.' "

Becky stared at her. "Oh, for goodness sakes! What's the matter? You were afraid your case was too easy for me? You wanted to give me a challenge? Now we have an impartial witness who can testify you were in possession of a document indicating that something pertaining to Matt Greystone could be found in a file."

"It didn't say 'Matt Greystone.' It didn't say which file."

"And it didn't say, 'Don't bother with a

trial, I'll just plead guilty.' But it might as well have. You now have the motive. The puzzle tells you the evidence you want is in the file. You break open the cabinet and find a file labeled 'Matt Greystone.' And the victim is so convinced that file is the reason the cabinet was broken into that she turned it over to the police. This case hasn't even started and we're already at the point where we should consider copping a plea."

"For what? This is not a capital crime. It's a robbery where nothing was taken. The only reason we're talking about it is because in this one-horse town it's the only crime going."

"The only reason we're talking about it is because you're the perpetrator."

"Well, if you're going to take that attitude."

CHAPTER 16

Cora was on her way to her car, which was parked in front of the library, when she heard someone call her name. "Miss Felton. Miss Felton."

She turned to see Matt Greystone's agent hurrying down the street after her. He bustled up, slightly out of breath, and said, "Oh, good, I caught you. I didn't get a chance to speak to you at the celebration. Of course, so much was happening. There's always such a commotion when Matt is around. Well, you can understand how it is. I was hoping we could have a little talk. Could I buy you a drink?"

"You can buy it, but I won't drink it," Cora said. "I've given up drinking. At least until my blood alcohol level returns to normal. I figure somewhere around the year 2525. Remember that old song? Or are you too young?"

"Well, I could use a drink. Could I buy

you a soda or iced tea or something like that?"

"Be my guest."

"Where's a good place?"

"The Country Kitchen has a sit-down bar. You know how to get there?"

"Can I give you a ride?"

"I'll meet you there. If you don't know where it is, you can follow my car."

"I know it."

The Country Kitchen had done its best to provide a rustic touch. The outside was designed to look like a large log cabin. The interior looked like an upscale country inn. The bar featured wooden barstools and wooden booths. Indeed, the theme of wood permeated the restaurant. Since she lived in cynical times, Cora wondered how much of it was real wood.

It being mid-morning, the clientele consisted of a few stragglers, no doubt trying to convince themselves a cold beer was the way to beat the heat. Cora had once embraced that theory, along with a few others of which she was less than proud.

The bartender was one she knew. It occurred to her she knew more now than when she was drinking.

"Hi, Ben."

"Hi, Cora. What can I get you? One of

these gentlemen?"

The bartender was kidding her. The gentlemen in question were a good twenty years her junior. And that, she realized, was a conservative estimate.

On cue, Matt Greystone's agent came in. "No, this gentleman here. I think we'll take a booth."

"Sure thing. Let me make you your drinks. I'm alone here, until Megan comes on for lunch."

"Diet Coke for me," Cora said.

"And a gin and tonic," the agent said.

Cora and the agent took their drinks and settled into one of the booths.

"So," Cora said. "I don't believe we were ever introduced."

"Oh. Forgive me. I'm Lenny Schick. And I know who you are. Everybody does. See, that's the thing. You're a famous person. Just like Matt. I thought maybe you could talk to him. One celebrity to another."

"It's hardly comparable," Cora said. "Matt is a huge star pitcher for the New York Yankees. I do TV ads."

"Exactly," Lenny said. "But you're not famous because you do TV ads. You do TV ads because you're famous. You're the Puzzle Lady. They're using your image to sell their product."

"I'm a media whore, is what you're saying."

Lenny choked on his drink. "Not at all. You're engaged in an honorable profession fulfilling a useful purpose. You're enlightening people about a nutritious cereal. It's actually commendable."

Since Cora didn't eat the cereals she was hawking, she was not sure how commendable that might be, but she wasn't about to argue the point. Cora wished she were somewhere else. Lenny Schick did not fall into her category of eligible males. She was not sure what category he fell into, but it wasn't that, and she sipped her Diet Coke a little faster.

Lenny realized he was losing his audience. "Anyway, it's going to be a tough year, what with the accident. It would be a tough year for anyone, but in particular for an athlete with limited shelf life. You work so hard to be drafted. And then you labor for years in the minors. And then it finally happens. You get called up to the show. And you're nervous as hell, and just hoping to do well enough not to get sent back down. But you're successful. Beyond your wildest dreams. You're a star. You sign a long-term contract for big money. You've arrived."

Lenny took a swig of his drink. "And just

like that it's over. Well, not over, postponed. Any person in that situation would be a fool not to make do with what he's got."

Cora sized up the little agent. "What are you trying to say?"

"If Matt can't pitch for a year he can't just curl up and die. He's gotta keep occupied. He's got to do something besides convalescence and physical therapy. He's gotta get out there, see people, let them know he's alive."

"And this relates to me being a, quote, 'famous person,' how?"

"The public has a short attention span. You gotta keep 'em interested. You've got it easy because your puzzles fuel your TV ads and your TV ads fuel your puzzles. Matt's just got pitching. And now he doesn't. Fans are fickle. A year's a long time. Matt should remind them who he is."

"You want him to do TV ads?"

"Why not? It's a win-win. It gets him out of his funk, it keeps him in the spotlight, and it keeps the money rolling in."

"That's a win-win-win," Cora said.

"Yes," Lenny said. He frowned. "Are you teasing me?"

"Just a little," Cora said. "You want me to sell him on the idea of doing TV ads."

"If you could just point out it's easy and fun."

"Obviously you've never done a TV ad," Cora said dryly. "I went on a publicity tour once. People tried to kill me."

The agent paled. "You don't have to mention that."

"Why not? It was the highlight of the trip."

A cell phone rang.

"Must be yours," Cora said. "I don't have one."

Lenny fished in his pocket, pulled out a cell phone, and clicked it on. "Hello? . . . Oh, hi, Jackie . . . I certainly could. As a matter of fact, she's right here." He extended the phone.

Cora took it, said, "Hello?"

"Hi, Cora. It's Jackie Greystone. Listen, Matt and I would love to see you. Could you drop by this afternoon about four o'clock?"

"I'd be delighted."

"Do you know where we live?"

"I've never actually been there, but I've driven by there."

"See you at four, then?"

"Sure."

Cora handed the phone back to Lenny.

"See, Jackie," he said, "do I give you service, or what? Was there anything

99

else? . . . Oh? Sure, I'll tell her." He hung up, said, "Wonderful woman. Strong-willed, fiercely loyal to her husband. A bit of a handful sometimes, but —" He stopped himself. "I didn't mean that. Like I say, a wonderful woman."

"What were you supposed to tell me?"

"Bring a bathing suit."

CHAPTER 17

Matt Greystone's house was an imposing structure built on a hillside by a New York zillionaire for his bride-to-be. When she ran off with an unemployed actor he lost all interest in the project, and put it on the market. It didn't sell. Way too pricy for a weekend retreat, it sat vacant on the south side of town, a giant albatross around the neck of the amorous young man, who barely deigned to acknowledge its existence. According to Judy Douglas Knauer, Bakerhaven's top real estate agent, offers were not pouring in, and her requests to lower the asking price had fallen on deaf ears.

The house was a huge embarrassment to Bakerhaven, owing to the manner in which it had been built. The zoning commission had accepted a donation for the completion of Bakerhaven's new rec center. The temporary relaxation of the zoning laws that allowed the rec center to be built had, in what was seen by no one as a mere coincidence, allowed for the construction of the mansion.

The house had sat vacant ever since, the only visitors the occasional vandal who hopped the low stone fence to check it out. These trespassers were usually teenagers indulging their curiosity. Most of them were caught, not that the estate had an alarm system. Despite the proliferation of CSI-type TV shows, none of the intruders had given any thought to the fact that they might be leaving fingerprints. In a depressingly typical learning curve, such failures had not made the teenagers more cautious in their intrusions, it had made them give up trying.

At four o'clock Cora turned in at the gate, and made her way up the long winding drive that cut through the majestic, sloping front lawn. In front of the building the driveway widened out into an impromptu parking lot. Nothing as formal as a circle or a square, it merely suggested a place to leave one's car. At the moment there were two. Cora joined them and made three.

The front door opened, and Jackie Greystone popped out. She wore sunglasses and a bikini that showed her figure off to good advantage. Mrs. Greystone was to all intents and purposes a dish.

"Cora, how good to see you. Listen, Matt's tied up on the phone. He sent me out to get you squared away. Come out back with me, will you? Four o'clock is the perfect time of day. The sun's not right overhead, but the water's warm. Did you bring your bathing suit?"

"I did," Cora said, tapping her drawstring purse.

"Excellent. Follow me. I'll get you set up." Jackie led Cora around the side of the house on an unobtrusive path of scattered flagstones of various sizes and shapes.

"It's good you're getting the lay of the land. Matt's throwing a party this weekend for some of his friends. Of course you'll be invited."

The back of the Greystone mansion was all beach house, including an in-ground swimming pool, a hot tub, deck chairs, cabanas, outdoor showers, a sauna, and a thatched-roof hut that served as a bar.

"Here you are," Jackie said. "Make yourself at home. You can change in one of the cabanas. I'll get you a drink. Would you like a lemonade? An iced tea?"

"I'd like a frozen margarita," Cora said, "but that life is behind me. Lemonade would be fine."

"A frozen margarita does sound better," Jackie said. "Would you like a *virgin* frozen margarita? I think I'll make myself one. Care to join me?"

"That would be wonderful," Cora said.

"Great. Why don't you change and join me in the hot tub?"

Cora went in the cabana and put on her bathing suit. It bulged only slightly in the wrong places. She was glad she'd taken off ten pounds. She'd put on weight when she quit smoking. She couldn't help it. She was hungry all day long. The only thing she wanted more than food was a cigarette. To start smoking again seemed counterproductive, particularly coupled with the depression and self-loathing that would have accompanied such a backslide.

What she could have used was a heavy-duty appetite suppressant, but since Dr. Barney Nathan, with whom she'd had a brief affair, had gone back to his wife, he was not about to write her a prescription. She'd have had better luck knocking off a meth lab, though it occurred to her that might not be good for her image.

Cora hung her clothes on the hooks on the wall, grabbed her purse, and headed for the hot tub. She dipped her toe in the water and found it pleasingly warm. She climbed in and sat on a shelf that submerged her up to her head and shoulders.

Jackie emerged from the thatched-roof bar with a pair of glasses and a pitcher of frozen margaritas. "Good, you're already in. Grab a glass and I'll pour you one."

Jackie poured Cora a margarita, then one for herself. She set the pitcher down and climbed into the hot tub.

Cora took a sip, proclaimed it delicious.

"Thanks," Jackie said. "Now, before Matt interrupts us, did you solve the puzzle?"

"It's in my purse," Cora said. "I'm not sure I can get it out without getting it all wet."

"What does it say?"

"It says to look in his file."

Jackie frowned. "What?"

"Hold on, it's a poem. I'm not senile yet, I ought to be able to remember it. Let me see. 'You'll find a surprise in the file of this guy.' "

"What does that mean?"

"I was hoping you could tell me."

"Well, I can't. A surprise in the file? What file?"

"The file of this guy," Cora said. "Which is all wrong, by the way. 'Guy' doesn't rhyme with 'surprise.' It would have to be 'guys.' 'You'll find a surprise in the files of these guys.' Except then there's too many letters to fit in the grid."

Jackie clearly wasn't interested in the mechanics of puzzle construction. "You said 'file of this guy.' Are they talking about Matt's file?"

"I have no idea."

"Well, it was sent to Matt."

"Yes, in which case it's telling him he'd find a surprise in the file of some other guy."

"Why some other guy?"

"Because he's not going to find a surprise in his own file. And he's not 'this guy.' He's 'you.' If it was his file, it would be, 'You'll find a surprise in *your* file.' Except there's no meter, it's the wrong number of letters, and it doesn't rhyme."

Jackie glanced toward the house. "Please. Before Matt gets out here. Can't you tell me what it means?"

"No, I can't. And the reason is I don't know."

"Well, what about the title? Untitled. Did you figure out what that is?"

Cora shook her head. "Not a clue."

Jackie took a breath. "All right, this file they're referring to. Could it have anything to do with the break-in the other day?"

"What break-in?"

"You know. At the house of that woman

people think is a witch."

"How do you know about that?"

"It's the talk of the town. Aside from Matt. Believe me, any time I can steer the conversation away from him I do. Anyway, the memory card was stolen from her computer, and a computer has files, so why couldn't it be referring to that?"

"It could, but she's not a guy."

"Maybe one of her computer files could be about a guy. As you pointed out, it didn't say 'files,' it said 'file.' 'Of this guy.' So she has a bunch of files and one of them is of this guy."

"I think you're doing a better job of figuring this out than I am," Cora said.

"I'm sure you've figured all this out already. I'm just trying to give you a prompt."

"Believe me," Cora said, "I haven't figured anything out. I'm not sure there's anything to figure." Cora took a sip of her frozen margarita. Her hand flew to her forehead. "Oh, my God! Brain freeze!"

Jackie laughed. "Yes, that is the danger of drinking these in the hot tub. Or anywhere else for that matter. Look, don't bring this up with Matt. He's got enough on his plate."

The pitcher himself came out the door in a bathing suit and a T-shirt. He wore a Yankees cap. His right arm was in a sling. "Sorry about that," he said. "I had a phone call. I try not to pick up, but there's some calls you have to answer."

He sat down on the edge of the hot tub and swung his legs into the water. "Ah, that feels good."

"Aren't you coming in?" Cora said.

"Afraid not," Matt said. "Doctor's orders. I do not get in the hot tub with anyone else, no matter how friendly. And that includes my wife. The fear is I would jostle my arm. I doubt if I would, but that's the fear. Lenny read me the riot act. The doctors were strict, but they've got nothing on Lenny."

"Not so hard to understand," Cora said. "You're clearly his most famous client."

"I'm practically his only client," Matt said. "Lenny's an old friend. Saw me pitch in high school. Told me I'd be good. Offered to represent me. I was flattered. A kid like me being recognized. So when I was drafted I honored his offer. It's not like having Scott Boras as my agent. But when it was time to make a deal with the Yankees he did all right by me."

"Well, you certainly made it easy for him, putting up the numbers."

"Anyway, I get in the hot tub alone."

"You want us to get out so you can get

in?" Cora said.

"Don't be silly. I use it several times a day. Enjoy yourself."

"Well, thanks for inviting me over. Lenny said there was something you wanted to ask me about."

"Oh. I'm having a party this weekend for some of my teammates. And some of my new Bakerhaven friends. You of course are invited, along with the chief of police, the first selectman, and some of the other Bakerhaven dignitaries."

"Did you say Yankees will be there?"

"They won't all show up, but they're invited. A few will come. Along with a few recently retired, such as Derek Jeter and Mariano Rivera."

Cora felt like she'd had another brain freeze. "Derek Jeter and Mariano Rivera are going to be here?"

"Well, I certainly hope so. Derek said yes. Mariano wasn't sure. And I'm not sure A-Rod wants to venture into Red Sox territory."

"I can understand that," Cora said, "but I'm a New Yorker born and bred. Derek Jeter, wow."

"So, I was hoping you could help me out."

"Of course. Anything. Just name it."

"Well, I'm new in town. I don't know

everyone. And we can't have an open house. We'd be overrun."

"I can understand that."

"So I was hoping you could help me with the guest list."

CHAPTER 18

"Kill me now," Cora said.

"It's a temptation," Sherry said.

"This is all I need. To be put in the position of choosing who's important and who's not. That's why we never have parties. So I won't insult who I don't invite."

"That's the problem with being a celebrity," Sherry said.

"It is. Though there's some people I'd *like* to insult. But there's others. Perfectly nice people. Friends of mine. But I can't force them on Matt Greystone, and they've got no reason to make the cut. And what a horrible position to be put in. It's like being an *American Idol* judge with no salary and none of the perks."

"You get to meet Derek Jeter."

"There is that," Cora said. "But, damn it, I'd like to meet him on my own merits, not because I was useful in making out a guest list."

"I understand your frustration. You gonna invite me?"

Cora's mouth fell open. "Sherry."

"You're not, are you?" Sherry said. "You're going to invite Aaron because he's a newspaper reporter, and Becky because she's a lawyer, and you're going to put them together in the hot tub and leave me at home."

"Sherry, you know I'd never —" Cora broke off at the look in Sherry's eye. "You're kidding me, aren't you?"

"What gave me away?"

"Nothing. You really sold it. I just realized that wasn't you."

"Good," Sherry said. "So how'd they like the crossword puzzle?"

"Well, Matt didn't see it."

"Why? It was sent to him."

"Yes, but it's his wife who wanted it solved. And then she didn't want me to bother him with the result."

"Was that after you told her what the puzzle said or before?"

Cora frowned. "As a matter of fact, it was after. What are you getting at?"

"Nothing. I was just teasing you again. I'd forgotten how much fun it was."

Aaron's car rolled up the driveway. He got out, went around, and lifted Jennifer out of her car seat.

"Mommy doesn't make me ride in a car seat," Jennifer protested.

"That's because Mommy doesn't blame Mommy for not doing it."

"Oh," Jennifer said. She hopped out, ran over, and greeted Mommy and Cora in turn, then raced to the screen door to let Buddy out. The toy poodle came pelting out and raced Jennifer across the lawn to the monkey bars.

"You're just in time," Sherry said. "Cora wants to invite you to a party."

"What party?"

"It's a pool party. You get to meet Derek Jeter and hang out in the hot tub with Becky Baldwin."

"What's she talking about?" Aaron asked Cora.

"There's a party this weekend. Matt Grey-stone roped me into helping him with the guest list. Sherry's come up with a scenario where I leave her off it and you hook up with Becky Baldwin."

"Sherry," Aaron said.

"Relax," Sherry said. "I was kidding her, not you."

"How is that kidding her?"

"Cora's freaking out about the guest list. She's afraid to make any executive decisions. It's a good thing she's not first select-man."

"Oh, my God," Cora said. "Do I have to invite the first selectman?"

"See what I mean?"

"I certainly do. Cora, stop worrying so much. Who's even going to know you made up the guest list?"

Cora's eyes widened. "Everyone will. That's the whole point. The Greystones can put anyone on the list they want. I'm not here to choose the guests they invite. I'm here to take the blame for those they don't."

Aaron grinned. "Oh, come on, Cora. It's just a guest list. Who could possibly care?"

CHAPTER 19

"You didn't invite my wife."

Cora nearly spilled her latte. She was barely in the front door of the police station when Chief Harper lit into her.

"Hi, Chief. And good morning to you, too."

"Good morning, hell. I get down to the breakfast table and there is my wife holding the morning mail, and guess what it is? An invitation to Matt Greystone's party. For me. And only me. And it's not just that it didn't invite the wife. It specifically says it's for only me."

"Oh, come on, Chief. Matt Greystone sent you an invitation and said don't bring the wife?"

"No. That I could deal with. But it's not a personal note. It's a printed invitation card. Mr. and Mrs. Greystone are pleased to invite, and then there's a blank where they fill in your name. At the bottom it says space is limited, no guests, please."

"Well, there you are, Chief. They didn't tell you not to bring your wife. They told *everyone* not to bring guests. It's not a personal snub. They just have limited room."

"It's an outdoor party. The guy's got acres. How much space is my wife going to take up?"

Chief Harper's wife had been filling out lately, as had he, but Cora managed to keep a straight face. "I don't know how many people he's invited, Chief, but if they all brought a significant other it would double the size of the party. Surely your wife could understand that."

"She might have, if she hadn't stopped into Cushman's Bake Shop because she has a weakness for their cranberry scones, and who's there but Judy Douglas Knauer, waving her invitation and crowing about how she's been invited to Matt Greystone's house."

"She's his real estate agent."

"Yes, and would you like to know the relative importance of real estate agents and police chief's wives? I could tell you, because I happen to be up on the subject for some strange reason."

"I didn't invite her."

"Did you or did you not make up the guest list?"

"Who said that?"

"Rick Reed. In his Rick's Rips segment."

"His what?"

"You haven't seen it?" Dan said. "It's a one-minute celebrity gossip segment someone at Channel 8 dreamed up."

"Sounds dreadful."

"It is," Harper said. "Anyway he comes on this morning with guess who made up the guest list for Matt Greystone's pool party and he named you. I thought it was funny until you slighted my wife."

"And Rick Reed is blaming me?"

"That's right. Is he wrong, as usual?"

"Oh."

"That's not the answer I was hoping for," Harper said.

"Matt Greystone told me he was new in town, and asked what Bakerhaven movers and shakers should he be sure to invite."

"I'm a mover and shaker? It's not funny, Cora. A lot of people are very upset and I'm one of them."

"How did Rick Reed come up with that?"

"I don't know. Did you leave him off the list?"

"He's not from Bakerhaven. Do you think I'd wish him on Matt Greystone?"

117

"Come on, Chief," Dan Finley said. "Give Cora a break. She didn't invite me either, and it's not like we're not old friends. I've known Cora ever since she came to Bakerhaven. I'm a big Puzzle Lady fan, and I was before I even met her. But she left me off the list, and it's not because I arrested her a few times or you wouldn't be going, either. So you've got to give her a break, because I know she's having a hard time."

"Thanks for your support," Cora said dryly. "What I want to know is how this all got tipped to Rick Reed."

"I have no idea," Harper said.

"You're usually his source, Dan. Are you saying you weren't this time? Despite the fact you felt snubbed for being left off the list?"

"Hey, did I say that?" Dan said.

"I'm asking you."

"No, did I say I felt snubbed? I don't feel snubbed. Apparently, I'm in good company. I mean, it's not like everybody and his brother got an invitation."

Harvey Beerbaum came in the front door of the police station. The chubby cruciverbalist was grinning from ear to ear.

"Hi, Cora. Thought I saw you in here. Hey, thanks for the invite."

CHAPTER 20

The young man at the gate had a clipboard and a Yankees hat. "Let me see. Grant. Aaron, Sherry Carter, and Jennifer." He turned to Cora. "I don't see you, ma'am."

"Because I'm not a Grant. My name is Felton. F-e-l-t-o-n. It should be above Grant, if your list is alphabetical."

The young man moved his finger up the list. "Hah! Cora Felton."

"Thank you," Cora said. "Are you with the Yankees?"

He smiled. "Batboy."

"I thought so. You've got that Yankee pride." She leaned her head in conspiratorially. "Can you tell me something? Is Derek Jeter on the list?"

The young man beamed. "He's already here."

"Then what are we standing around for? Come on, gang. It's a party!"

"Party!" Jennifer shrieked. She set off

across the front lawn with her parents and Cora in hot pursuit. All they needed was Buddy to complete the picture, but dogs were not invited.

Everyone else was. Cars lined the road in both directions. There must have been a hundred people there, but none were in front of the house. Everything was happening around back.

Matt Greystone's wife stood in the side yard, a recognizable beacon, attracting newcomers and ushering them around to the back of the house where the party was in full swing.

At least half of the guests were in bathing suits, though few were actually in the pool. One young man was doing laps. Another bobbed up and down in the water. One comely young lady in a bathing suit lay beside the pool, her wet hair attesting to the fact she'd been in.

"Wanna swim!" Jennifer said.

"With your life jacket," Sherry told her.

"Don't need a life jacket."

"No," Sherry said, "but you wear it anyway."

"Why?"

Sherry had a bathing suit on in case she needed to rescue Jennifer, but she wasn't planning on it. "So Mommy doesn't have to get wet."

"Ah, there you are," Matt Greystone said. He wore a bathing suit, T-shirt, Yankees cap, and a particularly bulky padded sling. "A compromise," he said, pointing to it. "The doctors let me have the party, as long as I look like I have no business going near it. Come in, have a drink, it's all informal. Lunch is a barbecue, eat anytime you feel like. Some people have to get back to the stadium, so no one's standing on ceremony."

"I'm not a big ceremony stander," Cora said.

"Cora, thank you so much for helping me out with this. If there's anything I can do for you."

"Actually, you can. Where's Derek Jeter?"

Matt grinned. "Don't worry. He'll find you."

"Huh?"

More guests were arriving, and Matt Greystone moved on to his duties as host.

There was a splash. Cora looked around to see Jennifer had plunged into the pool. Sherry sat on the edge, dangling her legs in, watching her little girl.

Cora looked around. For the most part, the guests were gathered in small clumps. The guests were largely segregated into Bakerhaven residents and Yankees. Cora didn't see anyone she knew. It had been years since she'd been to Yankee Stadium, and the roster had turned over considerably. Still, she watched TV, and she didn't recognize anyone. It occurred to her with a game that night, most of the people there were not players but Yankee brass.

The only one Cora recognized was Matt's agent, who appeared to be putting in double duty as a publicist and a bodyguard. While telling glowing tales of Matt's rehabilitation, Lenny always seemed to be on hand to block any gesture that might have jostled Matt's arm. Cora's assessment of the agent vacillated between gallant and desperate.

Cora headed for the bar.

"Cora!"

Cora's mouth fell open. The man descending on her was Harvey Beerbaum. The portly cruciverbalist wore aviator sunglasses and a loud Hawaiian shirt.

"Isn't this wonderful?" Harvey said. "Talk about upper crust. It's like the elite of the elite."

"Why, Harvey Beerbaum. I never would have imagined you to be starstruck."

"I'm not starstruck. It's just there's some baseball players you'd hardly ever see outside of a crossword fill. It's not like Mel Ott is here. I bet it never dawned on him

122

he'd be the most famous of them all. But A-Rod, there's a fill name."

"He's not here."

"Or K-Rod."

"Not a Yankee. But I know what you mean. Glad you're enjoying yourself, Harvey."

Cora turned around and found herself face-to-face with Derek Jeter. He wore a bathing suit and a Hawaiian shirt somewhat less loud than Harvey Beerbaum's.

"Cora Felton. What a pleasure. How nice to meet you. I'm Derek Jeter. May I have your autograph?"

Cora was overwhelmed. She blinked. "My autograph?"

"I'm a big fan. You know, a lot of us do Sudoku in the dugout. It's relaxing and sharpens the mind. Your Sudoku books got us through some long rain delays. Glad you got here. I can't stay that long, but I did want to meet you. And if you wouldn't mind." Derek Jeter thrust forward a piece of paper. "Could you sign this?"

It was a Sudoku.

"Oh, my goodness!" Cora said.

"I know," Derek said. "You must get this all the time. But I've heard you're a whiz at these things. Not just constructing them, but solving them, too. This isn't one of your

6						8		
4		3						
9	7	2			3	6		
7	6							
2					6			
			4	8			5	
	4		3		7			9
	9	7	1		4		6	8
				5		1		7

puzzles. I got this from a book by Will Shortz. I was wondering if you'd mind showing me how fast you can solve it. If you don't mind me watching you work."

Cora practically beamed. "Do you know how much fun I've had watching *you* work? Just hang on. You ain't seen nothing yet."

Cora whipped out a pen and zipped through the puzzle with a speed she hadn't displayed since the time Harvey Beerbaum challenged her to a Sudoku contest.

Cora signed the Sudoku with a flourish, and handed it over.

"There you go, Derek."

"Amazing! Thank you so much."

Cora was on the brink of proposing marriage when Derek Jeter was recognized and swept away by a throng of fans.

Cora bellied up to the bar triumphantly. "I'll have a Diet Coke with a slice of lemon."

"Livin' on the edge, are you?" said the bartender.

6	1	5	2	7	9	8	3	4
4	8	3	6	1	5	9	7	2
9	7	2	8	4	3	6	1	5
7	6	4	5	9	1	2	8	3
2	5	8	7	3	6	4	9	1
1	3	9	4	8	2	7	5	6
8	4	1	3	6	7	5	2	9
5	9	7	1	2	4	3	6	8
3	2	6	9	5	8	1	4	7

"You have no idea."

Aaron came over. "Well, my daughter can swim with a life jacket."

"I never thought she couldn't."

"I never thought she would."

"How'd you talk her into it?"

"I didn't have to." Aaron jerked his thumb over at the pool.

The witch lay floating on her back in the pool. She wore a life jacket. It was stylishly cut to show off the curves of her bathing suit, still it was a life jacket.

"See?" Aaron said. "Now it's a big-girl jacket. I won't be able to get it off her."

"This is why I never had children," Cora said.

"This is why?"

"Well, this and half a dozen time-proven methods of birth control."

"Did you get Derek Jeter's autograph?"

"No, he got mine."

"What?"

Cora floated around the party, lighter than air. A cluster of Yankee contingent caught her attention. Derek Jeter was elsewhere, and this was clearly another celebrity. Cora wondered who. She edged her way into the pack and stopped.

It was Becky Baldwin in a bikini. Becky looked good. Cora couldn't deny it. Becky always looked good, whether parading in front of the jury or simply holding down the desk at her office. But Becky Baldwin in a bikini at a Yankees party was a Yankee fan's trifecta. It was like the *Sports Illustrated* swimsuit issue come to life.

Jackie, who was standing watching, made a face.

"What is it?" Cora said.

Jackie jerked her thumb at the group. "Party crashers."

A middle-aged man in shorts and a sports shirt was insinuating himself around the periphery of the Yankee brass, trying to listen in.

Cora was disappointed. She'd thought Jackie was jealous of Becky Baldwin. "You know him?"

"Not really. Just a hanger-on. When you're famous there's always a group of people who pretend they know you. They're everywhere. That's the way these people work. They figure they're not worth throwing out. They're harassing you, but if you complain about it, you're difficult. It's better not to make a scene."

"He's harassing you?"

"He's a gossip columnist. Always looking to dig up dirt."

"It must be hard."

"It's all relative. Matt not being able to pitch is hard. Men like that are an annoyance."

Jackie moved off to greet some late arrivals.

Chief Harper came by. His wife was triumphantly in tow.

"Hello, Cora," she said. "How nice to see you here."

"Likewise, I'm sure." Cora lowered her voice. "Have you seen Derek Jeter yet?"

"He's here?"

"Right over there."

"Excuse me," Mrs. Harper said, and immediately transformed herself from policeman's wife into infatuated groupie.

"You brought your wife," Cora said.

"Damn right I brought my wife."

"How'd you manage that?"

"I RSVP'd that I couldn't attend because this afternoon was promised to my wife."

"And he said bring her?"

"That he did."

"You're a devious man, Chief."

"Thank you. Where's the bar?"

"That hut with the thatched roof. Are you drinking, Chief?"

"I'm off duty."

Harper headed for the bar, leaving Cora to look around. The man Jackie had identified as a gossip columnist tried to approach Matt, but Lenny deftly intercepted him and guided him away. Cora had a feeling it wasn't because the little agent was afraid he'd bump Matt's arm.

Over at the pool. Jennifer was rapidly turning into a prune. Sherry and Aaron's entreaties seemed to be having absolutely no effect on her. Cora had a feeling Jennifer wasn't getting out until the witch did, and that didn't appear to be any time soon. The woman was now floating on a rubber raft. She was lying on her stomach, displaying enough curves to do justice to your average Kardashian.

Cora smiled at Jennifer and shook her head. "Oh, baby, if you only knew."

CHAPTER 21

A booming voice split the air. "Where is he? Where is that malingerer? Come on. I've never known anyone to milk an injury so much. Get off your lazy butt and get back to work."

Matt Greystone's eyes lit up. "Oh, my God. It's the voice of doom. Don Upton. They let you out. And without a keeper. What's going on?"

The young man pulled off his sunglasses and smiled. "That shows how useful I am to the organization. We got a game this afternoon and they don't even care if I'm there."

"You started yesterday, didn't you?"

"You make it sound like I got knocked out in the first inning. I pitched seven."

"Where's the team today?"

"Cleveland."

"You came all that way?"

"I heard there'd be naked women. Where

are they? Where's the Girls Gone Wild?"

"Look in the hot tub."

"They have bathing suits. Don't you have a sauna?"

"It only holds four people."

"Me and three girls. Perfect. Hey there, young lady. I'm starting up the sauna. It's a bathing suit–free zone, feel free to join me."

Eyes swung to Becky Baldwin. Aaron looked in spite of himself.

"Aaron," Cora said.

"Huh?"

"It seems like a really good time to watch your daughter."

Aaron glanced over at the pool. Sherry looked up at him. "You and Becky are going in the sauna?" Sherry said.

"Don't be silly," Aaron said. "There's a waiting list."

Sherry's mouth dropped open.

Aaron pointed his finger. "Gotcha!"

Don was still carrying on. "You don't even have the sauna lit? What's the matter, wife won't let you? A ballplayer gets married and suddenly all the joys go out the window. Hey, Jackie. Your husband says you won't let him use the sauna. I'd rethink that. Lying around with naked women is the fastest way off the disabled list."

"You can start the sauna if you want, Don,

131

but I can't promise you any women. You'll have to scare them up yourself."

"Never been a problem," Don said. "Or was it drinking in the dugout that's never been a problem? That's the thing about being a starting pitcher. There's some days you know you don't work. Of course in Matt's case it's every day. How much are they paying you this year not to pitch?"

"Why don't you go fire up the sauna?" Matt said. He was still smiling, but to Cora it seemed a little strained.

"Let's see if I can scare up some wood." Don wandered off in the direction of the sauna bath.

Cora edged up to Jackie. "Who is that?"

"Don was Matt's roommate on the road when they pitched together in the minors. Matt got called up. Don didn't."

"A little over the top, isn't he?" Cora observed.

"Matt made it big. Don's still there. It's a tough situation. Well, you know. There must be crossword puzzle constructors who resent your fame."

Cora was sure there were. She could sympathize with them, since her fame was totally undeserved.

Jackie smiled. "Don means well, but I always have to watch him, or Matt will wind up on the front page of the *Post* with a top-less dancer in his lap."

"Boys will be boys," Cora said.

"Yes, they will. But my boy's news. No one gives a damn what Don does."

"Do you think he'll get the sauna going?"

"Unless he gets drunk and loses interest. Don just loves to provide fodder for the gossip columns."

"My niece's husband is a reporter for the *Gazette,* but he doesn't write gossip."

"What does he write?"

"Real news. Something has to happen for him to write it."

"As long as he doesn't make things happen. That's the sort of columnist who gives reporters a bad name."

Cora glanced around for the gossip columnist, but he didn't seem to be in evidence. After what Jackie had said, Cora could imagine him pawing through their garbage.

Over at the pool the witch was out of the water, and the Little Mermaid had taken over the raft. She seemed to be lying in the same pose the witch had. Cora couldn't wait to needle Sherry about it. She wandered over in that direction.

Aaron was nowhere in sight. Cora had a panic attack thinking she'd turn around and see him in the hot tub with a topless Becky

Baldwin. She spotted him easing his way into a group of men that included Derek Jeter. She wondered if he was angling for an interview. After having assured Jackie Greystone he only wrote hard news, that would be particularly embarrassing.

Chief Harper wandered by with what appeared to be a gin and tonic, but might also have been a Sprite. Whatever it was, he looked happy. He had also managed to lose his wife. Coincidence? Cora was making no judgments.

For the first time since she had gotten there, Cora couldn't see her host. It only impressed itself on her because he had been so aggressively hearty, as if to show everyone he was not bitter, he was a trooper, taking his misfortune in stride.

Matt's agent was gone, too, doubtless fending off countless conceivable foes.

The witch came out of the house. That was interesting, particularly with Matt gone. Had she gone in there to meet Matt? Or to spy on Matt? Or simply to use the bathroom? In which case, where was Matt? Or Jackie, for that matter? More people had arrived and it was getting hard to keep track of everyone.

No sooner had Cora missed her than Jackie bustled up. "Where's Matt?"

"I haven't seen him."

"Damn. I turn my back for one minute. Where's Don?"

"He went to gather wood. He's probably in the sauna."

"He's probably off with Matt, and that's not good. You let those two loonies get together." Jackie shook her head deploringly.

"It can't be as bad as all that."

Matt's agent seemed to think it was. He hurried up, wide-eyed, panicked, on the verge of losing it. "I can't find Matt. Is he off with Don?"

"I would say that's a pretty good bet," Jackie said.

"Doesn't he have any sense at all? That gossip columnist is snooping around."

"He's probably lighting the sauna," Cora said.

"You see any smoke coming out of the sauna?"

"I'll check it out," Jackie said. She headed across the lawn.

Lenny's eyes widened in alarm. "If Don's in there naked, don't go in!"

"Relax," Cora said. "Naked men are my specialty."

"Huh?"

"I'll handle it." Cora patted the agent on

the cheek and set off after her.

"Oh, my God, she went in!" Lenny said.

Cora quickened her pace.

Don came out of the woods with an armload of kindling. He was fully dressed, and not in the sauna. So much for that paranoid fantasy.

Jackie staggered out of the sauna. The door banged behind her. She clung to the frame, ashen and trembling.

Don dropped the load of wood and raced to support her. He took her in his arms, held her up.

Cora pushed by them and flung open the door.

It was a simple affair, two wooden benches, and an iron stove, the type that heated a stone that you poured water on to make steam.

The stone was not in its customary place on top of the stove, however.

The stone had been used to bash in the back of the gossip columnist's head.

CHAPTER 22

"I'm not a witness," Cora said.

The body had been examined and carted away, the crime scene had been cordoned off, and interrogations were in full swing. Matt Greystone had graciously allowed the police to use his house for the investigation, and questioning was being held in his dining room.

The witnesses were divided into three groups: those who had to be at Yankee Stadium at seven o'clock, those who didn't have to be at Yankee Stadium at seven o'clock, and Derek Jeter.

Derek Jeter was taken first, taken at his word, and excused. He had nothing to contribute to the investigation. He had heard of the man, but he had never met him, didn't know what he looked like, and had not seen him at the party.

Cora was surprised to find she'd been bumped up near the head of the list. After all, she wasn't starting that night in Yankee Stadium.

"Don't be silly," Henry Firth said. "We're all witnesses."

"Did you interrogate yourself?" Cora asked him.

Henry Firth made a face, which was unfortunate. Cora had always thought the county prosecutor looked like a rat, and it merely enforced the image. "You know what I mean. We're all witnesses, but some of us are more witnesses than others. You're a VIP in the Greystone household. You've had the confidence of both Matt Greystone and his wife."

"Neither of which would seem to be relevant," Cora said. "Matt Greystone had nothing to do with this crime, and I can't believe his wife did either. She happened to find the body. That's bad luck, but not incriminating. Anyone could have found the body."

"Anyone could have, but she's the one who did. She walks into the sauna, moments later she comes screaming out the door. The stone that had been on top of the stove is now on top of the victim's head. This is clearly a crime of opportunity. It would not have taken long."

"I'm sure Becky Baldwin would be de-

138

lighted to hear you just threw premeditation out the window."

"I'm not throwing anything out the window, and you know it. I'm just telling you how it looks bad for Mrs. Greystone."

"What does she say about it?" Cora asked.

"She doesn't. Becky Baldwin stepped in and made her clam up."

"Not before you had a good chance to question her."

"True, but nothing she said was particularly incriminating."

"Again I will relay the good news on to Becky."

"The woman claims she came in, found him dead, and raised the alarm. Not a unique defense strategy. What else is she going to claim?"

"I have no idea."

"But you do. You were seen talking to Jackie Greystone on several occasions. Witnesses saw you asking her something. You seemed to be indicating the decedent."

"Wow," Cora said. " 'Seemed to be indicating' is the type of cold, hard proof that sways juries. It's all right, Henry. I understand. Becky Baldwin is an attractive young woman. If you have a chance to throw some work her way it's gotta be hard to resist."

Chief Harper shook his head. "Please. Could the two of you stop sparring? This is tough enough without all that. Cora, do you know anything that could help?"

"I don't know anything that could help you make a case against Matt Greystone's wife."

"What was she telling you about the decedent?"

"Nothing personal. She just pointed him out as a party crasher. She said they're a problem. Matt gets besieged by hangers-on. And if he complains, he gets bad press."

"So she had a reason not to like him," Henry Firth said.

"Oh, sure." Cora rolled her eyes. "The guy represented a potential bad news clipping. If I had the opportunity, I'd have killed him myself."

"You were talking to Jackie Greystone just before she went to the sauna?"

"I don't know about just before."

"You didn't watch her walk across the lawn and go in?"

"No, I watched my niece's daughter swimming in the pool. Cute kid. Getting to be a handful."

"She's not the only one," Henry Firth muttered.

CHAPTER 23

Cora came out of the dining room and found Matt Greystone standing in the hall. "Where's your wife?"

"In the study with Becky Baldwin. I wanted to be with her, but they threw me out."

"They can't have a confidential conversation in front of a third party."

"Yeah, I get that. I'd still like to be there."

"So would I. Let me see if Becky will let me in."

"You're a third person."

"Yeah, but I've worked for Becky before. I can check if she needs me and see what I can learn."

"Do it," Matt Greystone said.

Cora knocked on the study door and pushed it open. "You need me?"

Becky looked up from the table. "Who said that?"

"I did. Trust me, you need me. Don't

worry about confidential conversations, you've already had one. Let's go over the stuff we can all talk about."

"Did Matt send you?" Jackie asked.

"No. If he thought to take this tack, he'd have been here. I told him I was checking up on assignments, but I'm happy for any news I can get. If you don't want me to tell him, I won't."

"That's fine, but I don't want you talking with my client. Her husband's another matter. I can talk with him. She can talk with him. It's the cops I don't want her talking to. But he's her husband. He can't testify against her. I just don't want him in here when I'm talking."

"What are you saying?" Cora said.

"Get him in here, and we'll leave the two of them alone."

Cora went out and found Matt Greystone. "Good news. Your wife wants to see you." She led him back to the study.

"Okay," Becky said. "Talk to each other all you want. If the cops come by, tell them to roll a hoop. Cora and I are going to plan your defense."

"Defense?" Jackie said.

"Potential defense. No one thinks you'll be accused of anything. But we have to prepare as if we did."

"All right," Cora said. "Why were you so eager to get me out of there?"

"What makes you think that?"

"You left them alone together."

"They're married."

"Becky."

"All right, all right. My client told me things in confidence I can't tell you."

"So you can't tell me?"

"Yeah, but if I don't I'll go nuts for the rest of the day and have a nervous breakdown."

"You have a sound legal mind. What's up?"

"She knows the dead man."

"She knows the gossip columnist? Who is he?"

"Leon Bratz, of Bratz Chats."

"That's the name of his column?"

"And his radio show. He has five minutes a day on some local station."

"And how does she know him?"

"He's written things about her husband."

"What things?"

"Like he's having an affair on the road."

"Does he name the woman?"

"He doesn't even name Matt. It's like

143

'What big-name Yankee phenom is doing better on the road than at home? He may not pitch every day, but word is he's getting quite a workout. One has to wonder if his wife has her head in the sand now that her bonus baby's hit the jackpot.' "

"What's your client say about that?"

"She says it's not true."

"She's with him on the road?"

"No."

"Then how does she know?"

"She says she knows Matt and he wouldn't do that."

Cora rolled her eyes. "Oh, dear. Another hopelessly naive young woman. You want me to talk some sense into her?"

"No, I want you to find out what this gossip columnist was up to. The stories he's published so far don't rate killing him. Besides, he's already published them, so you can't *stop* him from publishing them, you can only stop him from publishing *more*. I'd like to know what else he had that someone might not want to see in print. Did he get a confirmation on the affair? Did he get the name of the woman?"

"It's kind of hard to talk to him since he's dead."

"Yes, and isn't that convenient for someone who didn't want him talking?"

"Do you think the police might be of that opinion?"

"I can see them leaning in that direction."

"It would behoove us to find another suspect."

"It certainly would. Do you suppose you could circulate among the guests and see if you can scare one up?"

"Sounds like a plan," Cora said. "And I know just where to start."

CHAPTER 24

Cora found Don Upton hanging out by the pool waiting to be interviewed. As the man who was trying to start the sauna, Cora would have bumped him up the list, but Don was a minor leaguer and didn't have to be back to the stadium. As far as Cora was concerned, the Yankee brass didn't have to be back at the stadium either, just the players, and there weren't that many players there, but she didn't run the zoo.

"Hi, Don," Cora said. "Care to have a little chat while you're waiting for the cops?"

Don frowned. "Who are you?"

"You don't know me? I like you already. I'm Cora Felton. I'm known as the Puzzle Lady. I'm not famous enough to be here, I just happen to live in this town. I sometimes help out Becky Baldwin, the local attorney. At the moment Becky is engaged in making sure the police don't come to the erroneous conclusion that Jackie Greystone is responsible for the crime."

"I see," Don said. The young man had sandy hair and an endearing boyish grin. "She's the most likely candidate, and I'm the most likely alternative. And you're hoping I'll give myself away?"

"A confession would make things easier," Cora said. "The questioning threatens to go on all afternoon."

"Yeah, but I don't have to play tonight. And when you confess to murder there's always the chance of jail time. Which really cuts into a career."

"Anyway, you and Matt go way back."

"We were in the minors together. Before the trade. Shared a room on the road."

"Did you know the victim?"

"Not personally. I've heard of him. Everybody has. Good guy to stay away from. So I did."

"What about Matt?"

"Matt, too. No one on the team would give that guy the time of day."

"How'd he get an invite to the party?"

"You're asking the wrong guy. And there's no right guy. No one in his right mind invites Leon Bratz to a party. It doesn't matter. He just shows up."

"He's crashed parties before?"

"Sure."

"You've seen him?"

"Of course I've seen him. Everybody's seen him. A career killer, that's what they call him. He gets something on you, and then blasts you the moment you do good. Kid gets called up one day, gets three hits, with a double, he runs 'Guess what the raw rookie likes to hit besides baseballs? His girlfriend won't say, but she's been sporting a nice shiner lately. The newest Yankee declined to comment. Apparently getting a hit at the major league level makes a guy too big to talk to the press.' "

"You do that well."

"What?"

"Imitate Leon Bratz."

"Oh? You've heard him?"

"No, but I feel like I have. Tell me about the sauna."

"What about it?"

"You come in here, hot day in July, first thing you wanna do is start the sauna."

"I like to lie around with naked women. Is that so hard to understand?"

"No. When I was your age, I liked to hang around with naked men. Still do, actually. Like to, I mean. I think there's some morals clause in my Granville Grains contract. I sell breakfast cereal to schoolchildren. Not directly. In TV ads. Anyway, I'm wondering why Leon Bratz suddenly got so interested in the sauna. Was it just because you did?"

"I have no idea what he was doing there."

"Well, he was getting his head bashed in, of course, but that's probably not why he went. Why would he be following you?"

"I have no idea."

"I think you do. Otherwise you'd be trying to figure out why. But you're not even thinking about it because you already know." Cora smiled. "You know, you're very lucky you're getting this dress rehearsal before you talk to the police. You'll do much better with them if you survive me."

Don put up his hand. "You're starting to get strange."

"Believe me, you have no idea. Do you do crossword puzzles?"

"What?"

"Crossword puzzles, like the ones in the paper. Do you ever solve them?"

He shrugged. "Sometimes."

"Glad to hear it."

"Why?"

"The casual admission probably means you have nothing to hide. Would you know how to construct a crossword puzzle?"

"I don't know what you're talking about."

"And then that answer is the type you'd make when you do have something to hide.

149

It indicates to a trained interrogator that you know *exactly* what they're talking about, you just don't want to talk about it. It indicates to a policeman investigating a crime, for instance, that you know something about the crime they're investigating, and they'd do well to keep asking you. See what I mean?"

"No, I don't see what you mean. I said I don't know anything about constructing crossword puzzles because I don't know anything about constructing crossword puzzles. You can't understand that because constructing crossword puzzles is second nature to you, but it's not to me."

"Fine," Cora said. "Do you know anyone else at the party? You know Matt, you know his wife, you knew the victim. Do you know anyone else?"

"Well, Derek Jeter, of course. I mean I know who he is. He wouldn't know me. Oh, and what's-his-name. Matt's agent."

"You know him?"

"Of course. He's Matt's agent."

"Is he your agent?"

Don made a face. "I don't have an agent."

"So tell me about the sauna."

"What about it?"

"You went out there to start it. Did you go inside?"

"Yes, of course."

"What did it look like?"

"The inside of a sauna. Nothing special about it."

"You saw the stove?"

"Yes."

"What kind of stove was it?"

"What do you mean, what kind of stove was it? It's a wood-burning stove. That's why I was gathering wood."

"How does it work?"

"Are you serious?"

"Absolutely. Tell me how it works."

"You burn wood in it. It heats up the sauna."

"The stove heats the sauna?"

"Yes."

"It gives off steam?"

"That's right."

"Doesn't it take water to make steam?"

"There's a bucket of water by the stove."

"What do you do with the bucket?"

"When the stove gets real hot you pour water on it, it gives off steam."

"You pour water on it?"

"Yes."

"You pour water on the stove?"

"There's a rock. The stove heats the rock. You pour water on the rock."

"You saw the rock?"

"Yes."

"Was the rock on the stove or on the victim?"

Don made a face. "Was that supposed to trap me? When I saw it, the stone was on the stove. How it got on the victim I have no idea."

"Was there water in the bucket?"

"I didn't notice. Probably not. I doubt if it had been used for a while."

"Why do you say that?"

"That's not the sort of thing Matt and Jackie were going to fire up. Run around naked? Be a nice story for the gossip mags."

"Who could really care?"

"Not me, but I'm not famous. Hell, if I was, I wouldn't care. With everything that's been written about Matt, it makes him supersensitive. That's probably what what's-his-face was doing there, by the way."

"What do you mean?"

"Checking to see if the sauna had been used. 'What bonus baby pitcher's been running around naked on his estate? Rumor has it a Yankees star pitcher in rehab has a clothing-optional sauna.' Guy's nosing around, slips, hits his head."

"Right," Cora said sarcastically. "He slipped and hit his head on the underside of the rock that should have been on the stove.

I hope you have a better explanation for the cops." She pointed. "It looks like they finally got to you."

Dan Finley bustled up. "Sorry to interrupt. Cora, the chief would like to see you."

CHAPTER 25

"I don't mean to tell you how to run your investigation, Chief," Cora said.

"Well, that's awfully nice of you," Henry Firth interjected. "Would you mind passing that sentiment on to Rick Reed? I have a feeling that's exactly how he's going to report the situation."

"Don't worry. No one listens to him," Cora said. "Come on, guys. I was just talking to Don Upton, a guy who was actually *in* the sauna, and you haven't even given him a look."

"Are you kidding me?" Henry Firth said. "He was one of the first people we talked to."

Cora's mouth fell open. "He didn't tell me that."

"What?" Henry Firth said. "A witness failed to disclose to you that he had already had a chat with the police? That's shocking. Would you like us to proceed against him?"

Cora glanced from Henry Firth to Chief Harper. The chief looked uncomfortable. "Cora's only trying to help, Henry. Let's not give her a hard time. After all, she doesn't know what you have in mind."

"Why don't you tell her?" Henry said.

Harper still seemed apologetic. "We searched the sauna. Not that hard to do, but we had to get the body out of there. Barney Nathan was having a hard time examining it because there wasn't any light. It's not like there was a fire going or anything. Anyway, we finally got the body moved and we searched the place."

"There was something under the body?" Cora said.

"No, there wasn't."

"What about on the body? I trust you made an inventory."

"We did, and if there's anything interesting, we haven't found it yet. But we searched the sauna, and look what we found in the stove."

"What?"

Chief Harper passed over a plastic evidence bag. In it was a sheet of paper.

It was a crossword puzzle.

Across

1 Broadway bomb
5 Commercial: Abbr.
9 Like many zoo animals
14 Nash's "one-1" fellow
15 NYC cultural center
16 See eye to eye
17 Start of a message

19 Handy's "_____ Street Blues"
20 Top score, maybe
21 Opposite of FF on a VCR
22 Pinched pennies
24 Power source
26 Word of welcome
28 Frat members
30 Tubular pasta
32 Stage digressions
34 More of the message
39 Hawaii County seat
40 "Positive thinking" proponent
42 Titled woman
43 More of the message
45 "Hogan's Heroes" setting
47 Bitter _____ (purgative)
49 Last of a series
50 Problem for Pauline
53 Coaches give them
55 Coin's "tails"
57 _____ kwon do
58 Place for a mani-pedi
61 Tale of Troy
62 End of the message
65 Like snakes' eyes
66 Eurasian border river
67 Expensive wrap
68 Have a hunch
69 "Use by" info
70 Hobby farm occupants

Down

1 Fly like a moth
2 Valentine edging
3 Muscat's land
4 Give a thumbs-down to
5 WWII GI, e.g.
6 '50s music genre
7 Keydets' sch.
8 Tiny bits
9 Presidential appointees
10 G-man, e.g.
11 Prepare Parmesan
12 Angler with pots
13 Monopoly card
18 Sprang up
23 Gets taut
24 French red wine
25 2001's "Ocean's Eleven" et al.
27 Hawaiian fish, on menus
28 "Yeah, right"
29 Caron title role
31 Zero, in soccer
33 They may be cast
35 Either of two U.S. presidents
36 Crinkly vegetable
37 Online 'zine
38 Sonic the Hedgehog's company
41 "Green" prefix
44 Salon solution

46 Copier filler
48 Occupies, as a table
50 Martinique volcano
51 Bottled water brand
52 Enjoys a mystery
54 Cape Cod house feature
55 BBQ fare
56 Israel's Barak
58 Potato appetizer
59 _____ up (confined)
60 Is nosy
63 George's lyricist
64 Org. with a famous journal

CHAPTER 26

Cora found Sherry and Jennifer out by the pool. Jennifer was splashing in the water. No dead gossip columnist was going to spoil her fun.

"Where's Aaron?" Cora said.

"Trying to get a story."

"As if he didn't have a story."

"He's trying to get an angle no one else has."

"Oh, yeah? Well, I made a deal with the chief. We're outta here, if you can get the Little Mermaid to go."

Sherry looked over at Jennifer, who was spinning in a circle in the pool. "That may not be easy."

"They found a crossword puzzle. I said I'd solve it if they'd let us go home."

"You said *you'd* solve it?"

"Don't be unkind. I worded it so as not to out-and-out lie. The point is you and Jennifer can skip the questioning if we cooperate later when Dan Finley drops a copy of the puzzle off at our house."

"Chief Harper didn't want it solved on the spot?"

"It's in a plastic evidence bag, for which I am eternally grateful. Anyway, we can go. Aaron can come, too, if you can get him away."

"I doubt it. He's trying to scoop TV."

As if on cue, Rick Reed and a Channel 8 camera crew spotted Cora and descended on her.

"This is Rick Reed, Channel 8 News, at the home of Yankee phenom Matt Greystone, the scene of a grisly crime. I am talking to Cora Felton, the Puzzle Lady, who has just come from an interview with Chief Harper and prosecutor Henry Firth. Miss Felton, are there any leads?"

"I believe there are."

"Really? What can you tell us?"

"Oh, I can't tell you anything."

"I thought you said there were leads."

"Yes, but they're not substantiated. What we have are merely unfounded assumptions. And unfounded assumptions can be actionable if stated as unsubstantiated accusations."

Rick blinked, trying to wrap his head around the verbiage. "You're saying you

161

know who did this?"

"Absolutely not, Rick. And you can quote me on that. I have no knowledge whatsoever as to the perpetrator of this heinous crime. But I can tell you unequivocally that he or she is still at large."

"How do you know that?"

"Because no one's been caught."

Cora patted Rick Reed on the cheek, grabbed Sherry by the arm, and whispered, "Come on, let's get out of here before that genius thinks of a follow-up."

Chapter 27

"You're really leaving the scene of the crime?" Sherry said.

"Scene of the crime!" Jennifer said brightly. She'd graduated from echoing the last word of sentences to echoing as many words as she pleased. This was embarrassing for Mommy and Daddy more often than not, almost as if she planned it.

"I'm getting out while the getting's good," Cora said.

"I assume you're planning something devious."

"Devious aunt!"

"Hey, that's not fair," Cora said.

"What?"

"You didn't say 'aunt.' "

"So?"

"Now she's making things up."

"She's a smart kid."

"She's calling me devious."

"I rest my case."

163

"Case resting!"

"I'm sure she'll repeat that to Chief Harper," Sherry said.

"Chief Harper!"

"Or Henry Firth."

"Ratface!"

Cora's eyes widened. "You taught her that?"

"*You* taught her that. I told you to watch your mouth. So why'd you want to leave?"

"I can't tell you. Not in front of her. It's like talking to Rick Reed."

"You're comparing my daughter to Rick Reed?"

"Not at all. He's not even in her class."

"Miss Finsterwald's!"

"What?" Cora said.

Sherry burst out laughing. "That's the class Rick Reed's not in. Miss Finsterwald's. Jennifer's in it and Rick's not."

"Mommy said 'snot'!"

"Way too bright," Cora said.

"Seriously, why are we leaving?"

"I'm not saying in front of the kid."

"Suppose we use circumlocution?" Sherry said.

Cora gave her the evil eye. "If you start using words *I* don't understand, it's not going to help."

"No tough words. Just vague referents."

"You lost me already."

"Cora."

"Without alerting the local constabulary, I was hoping to solicit official cooperation in urban venues."

Sherry smiled. "See? That wasn't so hard."

CHAPTER 28

Sergeant Crowley looked up from his desk. "Uh oh."

Cora put her hands on her hips. "Well, there's a greeting. And uh oh to you, too, sir. I would think I deserved a little better than to be greeted as bad news."

Cora and Sergeant Crowley had been an item once until the strain of a long-distance relationship coupled with Cora meeting Crowley's on-again, off-again girlfriend, Stephanie, had changed the tenor of the relationship. Particularly upsetting to Cora was the fact she *liked* Stephanie, and didn't even have the satisfaction of wishing her slow and painful deaths. A refugee from the sixties, Stephanie sported flaxen hair, madras shifts, and ran a tapestry shop in the Village.

"So you're here to make trouble in my life?"

"Have I ever done that?"

"Have you ever done anything else? You're either trying to mess me up with Stephanie or get me to break the law."

"Which would you prefer?" Cora said.

"I got a homicide of my own to deal with, so I'm a little busy. You want to give me a hint?"

"Did you hear about the murder at Matt Greystone's estate?"

"The what?"

"You haven't. I'm surprised. Of course the gossip columnist who would be spreading the story is the victim, so I suppose it's understandable. But this poor communication between police departments indicates a degree of sloppiness that could come back to haunt you during an investigation.

"Here's the scoop. With the murder happening in Bakerhaven the police are concentrating all their efforts at the scene of the crime. But the victim happened to live in the City."

"You want to search his apartment?"

"Is that an offer?"

"Bite your tongue. If that's the reason you came here you're out of luck."

"It occurs to me if you don't want me searching his apartment, you probably don't want anybody else searching it, either. It would behoove you to sew the apartment up."

"Behoove me?"

"Did I use it incorrectly? I'm not very good with words, you know." Sergeant Crowley was one of the select inner circle who knew that Cora was absolutely hopeless with crossword puzzles. "Anyway, I thought I'd do my civic duty and alert you to the situation."

"So you hopped in your car and broke the speed laws just to warn me."

"We've meant a lot to each other. I couldn't let you go wrong."

"What's the real reason?"

"That's unkind."

"Sorry, but I do have this homicide of my own."

"Does it have a star Yankees baseball player involved? I'd adjust my priorities, Sergeant."

"Consider them adjusted. Well, it was nice of you to drop in."

Cora held up her hands. "Hey, hey, hey. Let's not be hasty. Telling you about the victim's apartment wasn't the only reason I'm here."

"I told you Stephanie's back."

"You have a dirty mind, Sergeant. I like that in a police officer."

168

"Cora."

"Okay, okay. Leon Bratz was a gossip columnist, wrote for a second-rate scandal sheet. He also had a radio show, five minutes a day on one of the AM stations. Of course he didn't do it live. Not the sort of guy you'd trust on live radio, even with a seven-second delay."

"So?"

"I'm thinking he probably had a little office slash recording studio to prepare his tapes and columns."

"Oh, you're thinking that, are you?"

"I'm thinking it largely because I Googled the guy and came up with an address on Seventh Avenue."

Crowley sighed. "Will nothing ever make you straightforward?"

"Getting what I wanted by being straightforward might, but that never seems to happen."

"So you'd like me to lock up his office, too?"

"Well, let's not be hasty here, Sergeant. You don't know if there's anything to lock up. And you don't know if he shares that office space with anyone else you'd be locking out. This is one of those situations where a knee-jerk reaction is likely to get you in trouble. Clearly this needs to be checked

169

out. If you're so busy, maybe your boy Perkins could run me over there with a set of passkeys. No reason to make a fuss if there's no fuss to be made."

Crowley scowled and snatched up the phone. "Perkins."

"Yes, Sergeant," Crowley's young officer said.

"Cora's here with a murder case. The victim had an office on Seventh Avenue. She wants us to take a look."

"Yes, sir."

"Hold down the fort here while I check it out."

CHAPTER 29

"Nicely done," Cora said, as Crowley drove his police car up the West Side Highway.

"What's that?" Crowley said.

"The switch. Acting like you were sending Perkins with me to check out the office and then going yourself. It's a classic reversal. The staple of many a mystery plot."

"You know why I did it?"

"Because you're interested and you want to see for yourself."

"No, because I'd never forgive myself if I got Perkins kicked off the force telling him to listen to you."

"That's less than flattering." Cora considered. "Accurate, maybe."

Leon Bratz's office was on Seventh Avenue just below 18th Street. Crowley left his car next to a fire hydrant and went up to the door. The building was a simple brownstone with no doorman and no lobby, just a row of buttons; 3C was labeled "BRATZ."

Crowley pushed it and got no answer. He whipped out a ring of passkeys.

"Wow, that's impressive," Cora said. "How do you know which one to try?"

"You try the easy way first," Crowley said.

He twisted the doorknob. The downstairs door wasn't locked. They pushed their way in and went upstairs.

Leon Bratz's office had a frosted glass door. Crowley knocked, got no answer, tried keys until the lock clicked open.

The decedent's office was slightly larger than a broom closet.

"Wow," Cora said. "What do you suppose this went for, fifteen hundred a month? Hard to believe it's an office and a recording studio."

The office had room for just one desk. On it was a computer. Attached to the computer was a microphone on a stand.

"Are these walls soundproof?" Cora said.

As if in answer, there came the sound of someone walking overhead.

"You really think he made tapes here?" Crowley said.

"Why not? It's the crudest of setups, but with a directional mike and a computer program he could record something good enough to pass."

"How would he get them to the radio station?"

"It looks like he's equipped to burn CDs," Cora said. "But I doubt if he'd have to. He'd just record the show and send it as an attached file or stick it in Dropbox."

"Uh huh," Crowley said. Cora sat down and clicked the computer on. The screen sprang to life.

"I thought you weren't going to touch anything."

"I'm not. That's why we're wearing gloves."

There was a battered file cabinet in one corner. Cora stood up, reached for one of the drawers.

Crowley stopped her. "What are you doing?"

"There might be a clue in his files."

"There might," Crowley said. He took out a roll of crime scene ribbon and began wrapping it around the cabinet. "And we're going to keep it that way."

"Spoilsport," Cora said. She flopped down in the desk chair. While Crowley was occupied with the file cabinet, she clicked on the email icon.

Leon Bratz's in-box filled the screen. The program automatically checked for mail and downloaded a cure for erectile disfunction.

Cora resisted placing an order. She clicked on Sent Mail. A number of the emails had been sent to the same place. Cora clicked on the latest one. It was his daily column. She skimmed it, but it had nothing to do with Matt Greystone.

Cora searched for his recording program. She couldn't find it. The man had so many icons on his desktop that searching for a program was sort of like playing Minesweeper. You clicked on one and hoped the whole screen didn't explode.

Cora had just spotted a particularly likely suspect, an icon in the shape of a tiny microphone, when something else caught her eye.

Sticking out of a slot in the top of the computer's tower was a tiny memory card.

Cora's pulse raced not unlike it once had when an irresistible heartthrob's wayward wife had come home unexpectedly. It was the wicked thrill of doing something wrong with the strong possibility of getting caught.

Cora sucked in her breath, and slid the memory card out of the slot.

"What are you doing?" Crowley said.

Cora hadn't realized her discovery had been audible. Smoothly she clicked on the tiny microphone icon. "I think I found his recording program. Yup, I did. Look at this."

"We have no right to listen to those," Sergeant Crowley said.

"I won't tell if you won't."

"Oh, no you don't," Crowley said. "Knowing you, you set that damn thing on record."

"Would I do that to you?"

Cora clicked on the most recent audio file. The voice of the decedent filled the air.

"I said no. Turn it off, shut it down, we're out of here."

Crowley herded Cora out and locked up the office.

Cora followed him meekly down the stairs, the memory card burning a hole in her purse.

CHAPTER 30

Cora roared up the driveway to find Sherry and Jennifer out on the front lawn.

"Hasn't she had enough sun?" Cora said.

"Tell her that."

"You think you could lure her inside for a minute? I need your help."

"Oh? You have the puzzle?"

"No, I don't have the puzzle. Why?"

"Dan Finley hasn't dropped it off yet. I thought maybe you picked it up."

"No, I need your help with the memory card."

Sherry's eyes widened. "You found the memory card?"

"Not *that* memory card."

"Whose memory card did you find?"

"I can't tell you."

"Why not?"

"I don't want to make you an accessory."

"Oh, give me a break."

"What's wrong?"

"You already told me about breaking into the witch's house. You weren't worried about making me an accessory to that."

"The witch isn't dead."

"Ah. You found the victim's memory card."

"I didn't tell you that."

"No, you skirted the fine line between out-and-out admission and non-implicating prevarication. I would say the odds of me actually going to jail are considerably reduced."

"Fine," Cora said. "If you're not interested in finding out what's on this guy's computer, I'll do it without you."

"Jennifer! Time to go inside!"

Sherry loaded the files from the memory card into Cora's computer. "All right, let's see what we have here. Well, we have a Word program with probably everything in it the gentleman ever wrote."

"It's a backup of his computer?"

"Not exactly. It's a backup of anything he's sent to it from his computer. Take, for instance, this file labeled 'Bratz Chatz #362.' This is a file from the computer, however, suppose he opened that file on his computer and made some corrections or added another paragraph. If he wanted the card to save his corrections, he'd have to tell it to. And then it would tell him there's another file with the same name and ask him if he wanted to replace it or if he wanted to save it as a new file under a different name."

"A simple yes would have sufficed," Cora said.

"And been inaccurate," Sherry said.

"Accuracy is a small price to pay for not having a computer lesson."

"Well, if you don't want help."

"I want help. I want help in the form of what's on the disk, not what conceivably might not be on the disk. I want something related to Matt Greystone."

"Well, why didn't you say so?" Sherry said. She opened a window on the computer, typed in Matt Greystone, and hit Search. "There you go. Ten separate entries about Matt Greystone. Would you like to read them over, or would you like to complain about how you're not learning anything worthwhile?"

Cora skimmed through the entries. They were, as Don had suggested, vague insinuations that weren't necessarily true. Matt's name was never mentioned. In all the columns, the name Matt Greystone only appeared in the titles of the files.

"Disappointing," Cora said.

"You were hoping for something salacious?"

"I was hoping for something helpful. How do you open the search window?"

"What do you want to search for?"

"Jackie Greystone."

"Control F."

Cora opened the window, typed in Jackie Greystone, and hit Search.

The computer lit up like a Christmas tree.

Cora read through the articles. Once again, the name never appeared except in the titles.

"Ah."

"Ah what?"

"Jackie Greystone was having an affair. At least, according to Leon Bratz. Assuming she's the unnamed woman appearing in the files conveniently titled 'Jackie Greystone.' "

"What are the dates on those files?"

"They're from this year. Largely February and March."

"In other words, during spring training."

"Yeah."

"Which takes place in Florida. Would Matt's wife go along with him on spring training?"

"I don't know. It's a lot of bus tours, and not much fun."

"According to these articles she was having lots of fun."

Cora frowned. "Maybe."

"What's wrong with it?"

"If this is true, how come no one else picked up on it? The other tabloids, for instance. They didn't get the story, he did. He may not have been big time but he certainly was busy and he came up with the dirt."

"So what? Why would the tabloids care? It's not like he copy-righted the idea. If the woman's having an affair, anyone could print it. And the *Enquirer* wouldn't be shy about publishing her name. They'd put it right on the front page. To all intents and purposes it would be their scoop. After all, Bratz Chatz never did mention her name."

"Well, there's the laws of libel, for one thing. You print something you can't prove, it's going to cost you a lot of money. They can't just make up stuff off the top of their head, they gotta have a source."

"They got one. Leon Bratz."

"No, they don't," Cora said. "Because Leon Bratz doesn't use her name. If he did, their article could be all about the fact her name appeared in *his* article. They'd sell it with the sexiest picture they could get, and the headline would be MATT GREYSTONE'S

WIFE IN STEAMY AFFAIR. They write about how she was named in Leon Bratz's article. He'd be the source. Their article would be all about his article, but they'd benefit from the headline and the picture and the fact they have national circulation and that headline would be screaming at people from the checkout line in every single supermarket."

"They couldn't run it anyway?"

"I don't know. I'd have to ask Becky Baldwin. I think it would depend on how his column was worded."

"All right, let's check them out. Who did he write for?"

"The *Tattler.*"

Sherry typed it into the browser. "How about that. They have a Web site." She clicked on the link. "Ah, this is convenient. We don't even have to be a member. We get a seven-day free trial. And they have an archive. That seems a rather elegant term for their type of trash."

"I guess they thought calling it 'landfill' would be confusing."

"Anyway, there's a search window."

"We can't search for Jackie Greystone if he didn't use her name."

"Yeah. Choose an article you want to search for."

"All right, how about this: 'What Yankee ace is honing his fastball in sunny Florida while his wife is working out in New York? Can you guess who's getting the most action?' "

"Let's try that one." Sherry typed "honing his fastball" into the window and hit Search.

There were no hits.

"Try 'Bratz Chatz 322.' "

"It won't be listed that way."

"It might."

Sherry was right. It wasn't.

"All right. Take away the number."

Sherry did a search for Bratz Chatz. There was a whole list going back about a year. The *Tattler* was a weekly. Bratz Chatz had nearly fifty entries.

"Okay," Sherry said. "The file was saved on February seventeenth. Here's Bratz Chatz column for February twentieth."

Sherry read the column. Cora read over her shoulder.

Sherry clicked the mouse.

"I wasn't finished," Cora said.

"There was nothing about Jackie Greystone."

"He doesn't use her name."

"There's no allusion to an unnamed pitcher's wife. Anyway, it's a whole different column."

The column for the twenty-seventh was no different.

Sherry and Cora checked out all the articles for March, then backtracked and checked out all the articles for February.

"You want me to try April?" Sherry said.

"It's not going to be there. By April spring training's over, he's back in New York, and he's already hurt his arm."

"How come there's no articles about him hurting his arm?" Sherry said.

"Probably because it's true. What's the fun in that? A rag like this gets no fun at all covering real news."

Buddy began barking hysterically and Jennifer yelled, "Doorbell! Doorbell! Doorbell!"

"Someone's here," Sherry said.

"No kidding. You could rent that pair out as an alarm system."

Jennifer ran to the window. "It's the police!"

"It's Dan Finley," Cora said. "Dropping off the puzzle. He better not be planning on waiting while I solve it."

"You can't. You have the whatjamacallit."

"What's the whatjamacallit?"

"I don't know. That's your department." Sherry opened the front door. "Hi, Dan."

The young officer came in carrying a manila envelope. "Did I hear your daughter yell 'It's the police!'?"

"She's our early-warning system," Cora said. "That's why we were slow answering the door. I was in the bathroom flushing our drugs."

"I got the puzzle for you."

"I'll run it back as soon as I'm done."

"That's not what the chief wants to hear."

"I can't run it back *before* I'm done."

"Yeah, look," Dan said. "The chief is not happy about this. We got a high-profile murder case. Rick Reed's footage is going to get national exposure because Matt Greystone's involved. The chief's gotta give him a sound bite that doesn't make us look like clowns. Anything you can contribute would be helpful."

"When's he going on the air?"

"It's big news. It's on the air all the time. On CNN the force looks none too sharp. We'd love to give 'em something to get them to change the breaking news banner."

"What is it now?"

" 'POLICE STYMIED.' "

"Don't worry, Dan," Sherry said. "We won't leave you hanging. Cora was helping me with something on the computer. We don't have to finish it now. Just let us log out and she'll be right with you. Sit down, take a break. Jennifer and Buddy will enter-

184

tain you. Jennifer, what do we say to the policeman?"

"You'll never take me alive, copper!"

Dan burst out laughing. "Thank you. I needed that."

"We'll only be a minute," Sherry said. She grabbed Cora by the arm and pulled her into the office. "Give me the puzzle."

Cora dug it out of the envelope. Sherry sat at the desk, grabbed a pencil, began filling in the grid.

"He's going to come walking in here," Cora said.

"No, he's not." Sherry set the pencil down, dashed out to the living room where Dan Finley was looking at his watch. "She'll be done in a minute. Can I get you something to drink?"

"I really don't have time."

"Hang in there, I'll urge her along."

Sherry darted back to the office, grabbed the pencil, finished filling in the grid. "There you go."

"Mind if I see that?" Cora said. "I should at least know what it says."

"Sure."

Cora grabbed the puzzle, read the theme answer.

"I CAN AVOID MISTAKES IF I CHECK HIS BRAKES."

F	L	O	P		A	D	V	T		C	A	G	E	D
L	A	M	A		M	O	M	A		A	G	R	E	E
I	C	A	N	A	V	O	I	D		B	E	A	L	E
T	E	N		R	E	W		S	T	I	N	T	E	D
		M	O	T	O	R		E	N	T	E	R		
M	A	L	E	S		P	E	N	N	E				
A	S	I	D	E	S		M	I	S	T	A	K	E	S
H	I	L	O		P	E	A	L	E		D	A	M	E
I	F	I	C	H	E	C	K		S	T	A	L	A	G
		A	L	O	E	S		O	M	E	G	A		
	P	E	R	I	L		S	I	G	N	S			
R	E	V	E	R	S	E		T	A	E		S	P	A
I	L	I	A	D		H	I	S	B	R	A	K	E	S
B	E	A	D	Y		U	R	A	L		M	I	N	K
S	E	N	S	E		D	A	T	E		A	N	T	S

CHAPTER 31

Cora burst into Becky Baldwin's office to find the lawyer closeted with her client.

"What's going on?" Cora said.

"Excuse me?" Becky said. "I'm in my office with my client. What's going on with you?"

"Was there anything funny about the accident?"

Jackie Greystone blinked. "Funny? Are you kidding me? It's the tragedy of his life."

"That's not what I mean and you know it. Is there any chance it wasn't an accident?"

"Hang on," Becky said. "You can't come in here and question my client. What the hell are you talking about?"

"The crossword puzzle found at the murder scene. The solution says to check his brakes. Is there any chance Matt's brakes were tampered with?"

"Of course not. Why would they be?"

"Did anyone check? After the accident.

Did anyone check his brakes?"

"I have no idea."

"Where's the car now?"

"It was towed away after the accident. I'm not sure where."

Cora snatched up the phone from Becky's desk, punched in a number. "Crowley, Cora. I need a favor."

"I just did you a favor," Crowley said. "If you need another one it means you're in trouble. Which means I'm probably in trouble. What the hell happened now?"

"Nothing like that. I'm just checking out a car accident. Beginning of April."

"April second," Jackie volunteered.

"April second. Single-car accident. Vehicle operated by one Matt Greystone. Can you pull the accident report, see if anyone inspected the brakes?"

"Why?"

"The crossword puzzle suggested it."

There was a silence on the line.

Cora covered the mouthpiece, said, "He's making up my eulogy."

"Aren't the Bakerhaven police doing this?"

"They may not have it yet."

"You held out on them?"

"No, but I may have beaten Dan Finley back to town. Come on, Sergeant, be a sport. Pull the accident report."

"I wish you wouldn't call me Sergeant when you're asking me to break the law."

"I'm at Becky Baldwin's," Cora said, and hung up the phone. "All right, let's talk turkey. Your husband was injured in a car crash. There is evidence someone might have tampered with the brakes. That raises it from an accident to attempted murder. People go to great lengths to cover up attempted murder. They even resort to murder. If someone attempted to kill Matt, the most likely suspect is always the wife. He just signed a multimillion-dollar contract. You won't get all of it if he's dead, but you'd get enough to be a very wealthy widow."

"Wait a minute," Becky said. "You come in here and accuse my client of murder."

"Not at all," Cora said. "I come in here and lay out the facts that might convince a misguided policeman that your client had committed murder. Now then, is there anything your client might say by way of explanation that you wouldn't want me to hear?"

Becky looked at her client. The consternation on Jackie's face told the story. "I better hear it first. Why don't you take a walk?"

"I'll be right outside in case the phone rings."

Cora got as far as the door before it did.

189

Becky snatched up the phone. "Hello? . . . Yes, this is Cora Felton's answering service. . . . Hi, Sergeant . . . Yes, she's right here."

Cora grabbed the phone out of Becky's hand. "What did you find?"

"I have the accident report."

"Just like that?"

"Perkins is very efficient. I'm not sure how he does it, but he does."

"Any mention of the brakes?"

"No. No mention of any mechanical difficulty whatsoever. The phrases 'misjudged the turn,' 'lost control,' and 'failed to keep the vehicle on the road' were used. The report places the responsibility for the accident entirely on the driver. There are no contributing factors cited such as weather, road conditions, or visibility."

"Did they check the brakes?"

"There was no mention of the brakes."

"That wasn't my question. Did the police check them?"

"Police don't check brakes. Mechanics check brakes."

"Did the mechanic check the brakes?"

"It's not part of the accident report."

"Why not?"

"If the mechanic had found something, it would be part of the accident report."

"Are you having Perkins follow up on this?"

"No, I'm having Perkins follow up on the murder in my jurisdiction. Would you like me to explain to you why that's more important than a three-month-old, nonfatal accident where there's no suspicion of foul play?"

"You're a sergeant, for Christ's sake. Can't you spare one officer to interview the mechanic? It doesn't have to be Perkins. You'd do it if Chief Harper asked you."

"Yeah, but he won't."

"Why not?"

"The accident was in upstate New York. According to the report, the car was towed to a garage in Rye. That's about as close to Bakerhaven as it is to here. I'm sure the Bakerhaven police will want to check it out themselves."

"A garage in Rye?"

"Yeah."

"What garage?"

CHAPTER 32

Bill's Body Shop was right off Route 287. Cora drove by the pumps and pulled up next to a rack of used tires.

In the first bay a mechanic was working on the underside of a Subaru up on a lift. Cora caught his attention, said, "You the mechanic?"

The guy looked at her like what did she think he was, a piano tuner?

"You work here three months ago?"

"What if I did?"

"I'd like to talk to you."

"Talk to the boss."

"I already did."

"You ask him if I worked here three months ago?"

Cora hesitated.

He grinned. "Got you. Yeah, lady, I worked here three months ago. And I'd like to be working here three months from now. Anyone wants to ask about work that's been done, they see the boss."

"Where is he?"

"In the store."

Cora went into the station. It was the type of place she dubbed an "inconvenience store," a service station with just enough soda and incidentals not to have anything you're looking for.

The man behind the counter was watching a small TV on the wall. It looked like the monitor from a surveillance system. A loose wire hung in a loop from the TV out the side window. Cora figured the guy was stealing cable from the house next door.

"What can I do for you?" the guy said.

The garage was one of those places where you prepay for gas. He clearly expected her to say something like, "Put twenty dollars on pump three."

"I'm investigating an accident," Cora said.

The guy could not have looked more surprised if she hit him over the head with a shovel. "What accident?"

"You had a car towed here three months ago."

"I have a lot of cars towed in here. That's what we do."

"This one you'd remember."

"Why?"

"It belonged to Matt Greystone."

193

"Yeah, that was a shock. No one said nothing, then I look at the name on the registration. They said to check it for mechanical failure. That's a joke."

"Why?"

"Head-on collision. Car's a twisted wreck. You could tell if a tire blew, but whether it caused the accident or was the result of it is hard to say. No, you list the damage. Then you come in later with your cops and your lawyers and your insurance adjusters. And if the car hasn't been hauled off for junk you can inspect it again."

"Were the brakes cut?"

"What?

"The brake hoses. Were they cut?"

"If the cables had been cut, Donnie would have said so."

"Did he check?"

"Of course he checked?"

"Why? Are cut brake hoses a common cause of accidents?"

"Look, lady, you want to ask questions, fine. You don't like the answers, I'm not going to argue with you."

"Where's the car now?"

"Out back."

"It's still here?"

"He didn't want it repaired, he just wanted it junked. We're a body shop. The rear end's in good condition, I can use it for parts."

"Did you sell the brakes?"

"Don't get a lot of calls for used brakes."

"So you could check them now."

"I could, but I'm not gonna."

"Why not?"

"Because no one's paying me to."

"Fair enough. A hundred bucks if you do it right now."

"That's not a lot of money."

"No, but it's what you can get. When the police show up you'll have to do it, and you won't get a dime."

He came out from behind the counter, banged out the door, and walked over to the service bay. "Hey, Donnie. Pull the Greystone car in here and check the brakes."

Donnie looked surprised. "I'd have to put it on the lift."

"So put it on the lift."

"There's a car on the lift."

"Take it down. When you get it up there, see if the brake lines have been cut."

"Why would the brake lines be cut?"

"They wouldn't. So check if they are, and tell the lady what we already know."

Donnie jerked his thumb at the car on the lift. "I'll have to put the tires back on."

"I don't care how you do it, just get it done."

Donnie looked at Cora as if she were something he had just scraped off his shoe. He grabbed an air gun and bolted the tires back on with lug nuts. For all his bellyaching it took about two minutes. He lowered the lift, backed the car off, hopped in the wrecker, and towed the Greystone car around. The only hard part was backing it onto the lift. He accomplished it with insolent skill, unhooked the tow truck, lifted the wreck in the air.

He walked under the car and pointed. "The brakes are intact. They're the original brakes. They're in pretty good shape, but they won't sell, no one's looking to buy used brakes. Here's the brake lines. If you were gonna, you'd cut 'em here. As you can see, no one did."

"What about the rest?"

Donnie checked out the brakes. He didn't skimp the job. There was hostility in his thoroughness. Every gesture seemed to say, see, lady?

"How about the brake lines themselves. Have they been replaced?"

"Sure, lady, after I inspected the car someone snuck in here in the dead of night, put it up on the lift, took off the cut brake line, and replaced it with a new one."

"Could that have happened?"

196

"No. These are not new brake lines, these are the original brake lines that came with the car. Look, I don't know what dog you have in this race, but whatever your interest, the answer is the same."

Donnie pointed at the car on the lift. "These brakes have never been tampered with."

CHAPTER 33

Chief Harper was fit to be tied. "I ought to run you in."

"Gee, Chief," Cora said. "I solve a crossword puzzle for you and this is the thanks I get."

"You're meddling in a police investigation."

"What investigation? I'm not even up on your investigation. Any progress in the Matt Greystone case?"

"I sent Dan Finley down to Rye, New York, to check out Matt Greystone's car. What do you think he found?"

"The car?"

"He found two very cranky service station guys who weren't the least bit interested in checking Matt Greystone's car because they said some little old lady had already had them do it."

"That's just hurtful, Chief, assuming they meant me. Little old lady indeed."

"Did you pay them a hundred dollars to check out Matt Greystone's brakes?"

"Would that be a crime?"

"That's not the question. The question is did anyone tamper with the brakes. The answer is yes. You did. Before the police could inspect them."

"That's a rather harsh way of describing it."

"Not as harsh as how the prosecutor describes it. Not only did you tamper with the brakes, but the police department *let* you tamper with the brakes."

"This is getting far afield, Chief. Just because a crossword puzzle says something doesn't mean it has anything to do with your crime. You're not investigating a single-car accident, you're investigating a murder."

"I'm investigating the murder of a gossip columnist. I'm looking for a motive. Covering up a prior murder attempt works just fine."

"Oh, your theory is someone tried to kill Matt Greystone, the gossip columnist got wind of it so someone bumped him off?"

"What's wrong with that?"

"Oh, a few holes here and there."

"This isn't rocket science, Cora. The wife stands to inherit, and the wife was discovered with the dead body."

"The wife *discovered* the dead body, Chief. Do you have enough to pick Jackie Greystone up?"

"Not my call."

"Does Ratface think you have enough to pick her up?"

"Henry Firth has a horror of prosecuting the wrong man."

"Once bitten, twice shy?"

"It's embarrassing to start prosecuting a suspect and then find out you have more evidence against someone else. He's gonna be damn sure that doesn't happen this time."

"Good to know. I'll tell Becky she's on firm ground saying, 'Charge her or release her.'"

Harper made a face. "Couldn't we do this without so much sparring?"

"You're the one who accused me of meddling in a police investigation."

"You're the one who meddled." Harper sunk back in his desk chair, ran his hand over his forehead. "You know, the air-conditioning in here could work better."

"Why don't you get it fixed?"

"I put in a requisition."

"A requisition? Is this what it's come to, Chief, everything in triplicate? You're the chief of police. Call the repairman or replace the damn thing."

Harper heaved a huge sigh. "I got a crossword puzzle says check the brakes. There's nothing wrong with the brakes. So what the hell was the crossword puzzle all about?"

"Maybe it has nothing to do with the killing."

"It was found at the scene of the crime."

"Maybe it meant another car."

"What other car? That's the only accident even remotely connected."

"Did you check Leon Bratz's car?"

"No. Why would I check that?"

"It's remotely connected."

"Leon Bratz didn't have an accident. Someone bashed his head in."

"Yeah, but if they hadn't. If he'd taken his car home, would he have driven off the road?"

Harper snatched up the phone. "Dan. Find out where Leon Bratz's car is. Have it towed in and check it out from top to bottom. Put an emphasis on the brakes." He hung up the phone, looked at Cora. "You think that's the answer?"

Cora grimaced. "Chief, I don't even know the question."

"Do you think the victim's brakes were tampered with?"

"I think it's a hundred to one shot. But you ask me whose other brakes it could be, and that's who I come up with. Of course if Jackie Greystone drives into a large tree, I'll revise my estimate."

"Do you think the suspect was the intended victim?"

"I don't think anything, Chief. You're asking me for possible scenarios."

"Yeah, well how about giving me probable ones."

Dan Finley burst in the door. "Matt Greystone just drove his car off the road!"

CHAPTER 34

Chief Harper screeched his car to a stop at the side of the road and he and Cora leapt out.

The rear of Matt Greystone's car protruded from a ditch. Matt's agent, Lenny Schick, stood talking to Judy Douglas Knauer, whose blue Nissan was pulled up alongside.

"Where's Matt?" Cora demanded.

"He's home," Lenny said.

"You sent him home?" Chief Harper said.

"I left him home. The party had to be a strain. No reason to be up and about."

"He drove his car into a ditch," Harper said.

"Don't be silly. *I* drove his car into a ditch. Not my fault, really. I put on the brakes and nothing happened."

"The brakes failed?"

"It certainly looks like it. Good thing it was me driving and not Matt. He couldn't

203

have handled it with one arm. I could barely do it with two. I was okay until it picked up speed on the grade. I'd have made it, but the car knocked me sideways on the S-turn. By the time I straightened up I was in the ditch."

"You're saying you drove his car?"

"Sure. I took his car to town because it was blocking mine. Everything seemed fine until I hit the downgrade. I stepped on the brake and the pedal went right to the floor."

"You're not hurt?"

"I'm not. How do you like that? The deepest pockets in the world and I can't even sue." He put up his hand. "Don't call me on that. I may have some back injury that pops up later."

Cora pulled Judy aside. "You saw the accident?"

"I phoned it in."

"But you saw it happen?"

"I came along right after. The car was off the road. He was just climbing out of the ditch. I called the station, spoke to Dan Finley. You guys sure got here fast."

"So you didn't actually see the car go off the road?"

"No."

"Did you hear the crash?"

"No, but what's to hear? It's not like it

smashed into anything. It just got stuck in a ditch."

"Headfirst."

"Yeah, but I don't think it's that bad. The front isn't caved in or anything. And Lenny got out the front door. He didn't have to kick a window open."

Chief Harper came over. "What are you doing?"

"Talking to Judy. She's the one who called it in."

"What's she been asking you?"

"If I saw the car go off the road. Which I didn't. It must have been just before I got there. As soon as I saw it, I pulled off the road and called it in."

"That's what I was telling her, Chief. If only more people were civic minded."

Chief Harper pulled Cora away. "What's your angle?"

"Angle?"

"You come to a car crash, you don't want to look at the car, you don't want to talk to the driver, you're interested in the person who called it in."

"Judy's a bridge partner."

"I'm going to make every effort to co-operate with Becky in terms of her repre-senting her client, as long as cooperation is a two-way street. What are you getting at?"

205

"It's mighty convenient Matt's agent is the one driving the car when it went off the road. The guy's desperate to control publicity, he's been trying to put a positive spin on Matt's injury. If Matt wasn't up to driving his car, that might be the sort of thing his agent might want to suppress.

"Dan Finley said Matt Greystone drove his car off the road. So that's what Judy must have told him. Now she says his agent drove his car off the road. I'm just wondering why she changed her mind."

Chief Harper strode back to Judy Douglas Knauer. "When you called Dan Finley, didn't you say Matt Greystone drove off the road?"

"Yes. Because I recognized the car."

"But you didn't see him?"

"No. But I knew the car pretty well. I showed them enough houses before they settled on that one."

"When did you see Lenny Schick?"

"When I stopped my car and got out he was climbing up the bank."

"And the accident had just happened?"

"It must have. He wouldn't have sat down there waiting for me to come along."

Chief Harper looked at Cora. She could tell that was exactly what he was thinking.

Harper jerked his phone out of his pocket.

"Dan, cancel the ambulance. Matt Grey-stone wasn't in the car. His agent drove it off the road. He's fine. He says the brakes failed. Have it hauled in and check the brakes."

Harper clicked the phone off. "Let's go talk to Matt."

CHAPTER 35

Matt Greystone was concerned. "Are you all right?" he asked Lenny. "Shouldn't a doctor check him out?"

"Relax, I'm not going to sue," Lenny said.

Matt looked shocked. "I never thought you were."

"I'm joking. To let you know I'm all right."

"Why'd you take Matt's car?" Jackie said.

"Mine was blocked in."

She frowned.

"You haven't been out today?" Harper asked Matt.

"No. With everything that happened, I didn't need the excitement and I didn't want to talk to the press."

"They've been calling all day," Jackie said. "We stopped answering the phone. And there's a news van lying in wait for us. They were parked at the end of the driveway until one of your officers shooed them away. I saw him from the upstairs window. He wasn't subtle about it."

"Ah, that would be Sam Brogan," Harper said. "He has his own way of doing things."

Cora smiled. The cranky Bakerhaven officer was not noted for his patience.

"He chased them back to town," Jackie said. "But if Matt went out, they'd be all over him."

"As a celebrity, you must be used to that," Harper said.

"As a *pitcher,* I'm used to that," Matt said. "I can stand in front of reporters who want to know why I left a fastball over the middle of the plate and gave up a three-run homer. I don't know how to answer questions about a murder. I don't know anything about it and I don't know what to say."

"That would do just fine," Cora said. "Trust me, I've been in your position. Well, not exactly, I'm not that famous, but I've been in the position of people wanting me to explain a murder when I haven't a clue." She jerked her thumb at Chief Harper. "He's asked me more than once. It's no fun, but I've gotten used to it. And, trust me, you'll do very well with your humble sincerity. If you can fake that, you're home free."

Matt's head snapped up defiantly.

Chief Harper jumped in before Cora completely hijacked the conversation. "What are all the cars out front?"

"Oh, the cleanup crew and the caterers."

"The caterers are still here?"

"That's your fault. Your officers wouldn't let them take anything away. The place was a crime scene."

"The sauna still is."

"I know. The crime scene ribbon's still up."

"Make sure no one goes in there."

"We won't. I can't promise some tres-passer won't go in there."

Chief Harper didn't look pleased at that, but realized there was nothing he could do about it. "When is the last time you drove your car?"

"I can't drive. I have to have people drive me."

"When's the last time *anyone* drove the car?"

"Boy, I'd have to think back," Matt said. "Let's see, we went out two days ago, but that was in Jackie's car."

"If you don't drive, how'd your car get here?" Harper said. "You've got two cars. Your wife drove her car. Who drove yours?"

Matt looked at Jackie, looked at Lenny, and shrugged. "Got me. I drove it up here. Very slowly, and very carefully, but I like to have a car. Like you say, Jackie couldn't drive it up. I suppose I could have hired a driver, but then I'd have to get rid of him."

"You didn't tell me that," Lenny said.

Matt grimaced. "See? Now you got me in trouble with my agent. No, I didn't tell you that because you'd have had a nervous breakdown. It's hard enough with one of us out of commission. I need you doing what you do."

"But I'm not doing it," Lenny said. "I'm running around playing nursemaid to a naughty child."

"So," Harper said, "if someone sabotaged the brakes, would they have a reasonable expectation that you would be driving the car?"

"They'd have no reason to expect that I *wouldn't,*" Matt said. "Lenny's seen to that. He's obsessive about it. Any indication that I wasn't up to doing something, anything at all, and he's falling all over himself proving it isn't true. He doesn't want me to drive, and he doesn't want anyone to know I'm not driving."

Harper's phone rang. He grabbed it. "Yeah?" He listened a while, said "Thanks," and clicked it off. "The car's on the way to the garage. It doesn't appear to be damaged, but the mechanic's going to check it out."

"What garage?" Matt asked.

"Hank Farley's place. Mobil station north of town. Don't worry, they'll call you. If driving it is a problem, I'm sure they can arrange to deliver."

"Great."

"So, getting back to the last time the car was driven."

"Don't look at me," Matt said. "I haven't driven it since it's been up here. I swear to God, Lenny."

"I took it to the store the other day," Jackie said.

"Why, if you have your own car?" Harper said.

"I like to drive it."

"If you want a car like mine, we can get you a car like mine," Matt said. "I thought you liked your car."

"I do. Sometimes I like to drive yours."

Harper put up his hand. "And when would that have been that you drove the car?"

Jackie bit her lip. "I would say Wednesday or Thursday. Best I can do. I can't think of anything to tie it down."

"Any trouble with the brakes?"

"No."

"Did the pedal go all the way to the floor?"

"I'm sure I would have noticed that."

"And the car didn't buck when you put on the brakes, like you were on a bumpy road?"

"No, nothing like that. I tell you, there was no problem."

Jackie took Cora by the arm. "Cora, let's give these men some space. Come help me in the kitchen."

"Sure," Cora said. She followed Jackie Greystone out of the room. "Now, what am I helping you with?"

"That's a euphemism for get the hell out of here."

"I thought it was. Men used to retire to the drawing room for brandy and cigars. Women could get away from them. Now we have to make up excuses. What is it now?"

"The puzzle."

"I solved the puzzle."

"I got another puzzle."

"Really?"

"Really." Jackie pulled an envelope out of her purse. "And this one's titled."

"What's the title?"

" 'Matt.' "

"Uh oh," Cora said.

Across

1 "Just the facts, _____ !"
5 Brussels-based alliance
9 Totally destroy
14 Jessica of "Dark Angel"
15 Like much folklore
16 Three-line verse

17 Start of a message
19 Conclude with
20 Parlor pieces
21 "Madame X" painter John Singer
   _____
23 _____ out (distribute)
25 Charlotte of "The Facts of Life"
26 Bowie's last stand
30 More of the message
35 Casaba and Crenshaw
37 Airline seat part
38 Fort _____, N.J.
39 Plugging away
40 Itsy-bitsy
42 Napoleon victory site of 1796
43 "_____ the season . . ."
44 Place for a cooling pie
45 T-shirt sizes
47 More of the message
50 Sports shocker
51 The whole shebang
52 Chuckwagon fare
54 Like canned nuts
58 Fill to excess
63 Goodie from Linz
64 End of the message
66 Hot to trot
67 Twistable treat
68 Without peer
69 Cattle zappers

70 Farmyard female
71 "Zounds!"

Down

1 Baseball's "Say Hey Kid"
2 Shaving gel additive
3 Touch on
4 Brewer's ingredient
5 Checking account come-on
6 Whitney Houston's longtime record label
7 Sunbather's goal
8 Car make until 2004, for short
9 Rehab treatment
10 Yellowstone employee
11 Intern, e.g.
12 Onion cover
13 Seek prey
18 Polish scent
22 Orderly groupings
24 Parsons of "Bonnie and Clyde"
26 Treasured violin
27 Allow to enter
28 Elite invitees
29 Witty rejoinder
31 Starbucks vessel
32 Ones on pedestals
33 Move like a crab
34 Live and breathe

36 Stop, as a yawn
41 One of the Mannings
42 400-meter path, perhaps
44 Some eBay users
46 "Is that an order?"
48 Put the kibosh on
49 Parade time
53 Truckee River feeder
54 Part of a flight
55 Winter coating
56 "In which case . . ."
57 Dire prophecy
59 Skye, for one
60 Bug-eyed
61 Ahi, e.g.
62 Gave the once-over
65 Address for a monk

"Yeah."

"All right, hand it over. I'll take it home and solve it."

"You're not going to solve it here?"

"Not unless you want Chief Harper to get it." Cora took the envelope and thrust it into her drawstring purse.

"You're not even going to look at it?"

"What good would that do?"

"Something might occur to you."

Nothing had ever occurred to Cora while looking at a crossword puzzle except the fact it was giving her a headache and she wished she were someone else.

"I'll look at it when I get home. Right now I'm not entirely comfortable leaving your husband alone with Chief Harper and that agent. He might say something he shouldn't."

"How could that happen?"

"Trust me, there's ways," Cora said. "Right now I'm trying to make sure you don't find out."

Cora got back in the other room to find Chief Harper giving Matt Greystone a hard time. At least she could infer that from the fact Matt's agent was on his feet and had moved in between the two of them, and Chief Harper was attempting to placate him.

"You're too quick to take offense," Chief Harper said. "Yes, I changed the subject to the murder. The murder took place on this property, and is as yet unsolved. I'm sorry you think it's unfair I should bring it up, but, trust me, it's a legitimate topic for conversation."

"My client clearly doesn't want to talk about it," Lenny said.

"I didn't say I didn't want to talk about it," Matt protested.

"You were getting pissed," Lenny said. "Trust me, I can tell when you're pissed.

And I quite understand it. You haven't had a particularly easy time."

"No one's trying to give anyone a hard time," Harper said. "We'd love to get out of your hair as soon as possible. Believe me, that's all I'm trying to do."

"Yeah, yeah, I know," Matt Greystone said. "I don't mean to be cranky, Chief, but I'd feel a lot better about this whole thing if you could come up with any suspect other than my wife."

Harper sighed. "So would I."

CHAPTER 36

"I got another one," Cora announced.

Sherry looked up from the stove where she was stirring a lamb stew. "Too general. Another boyfriend? Another ex-husband? Another bad habit?"

"Is that nice?"

"Well, if you're going to set me up like that."

"I got another crossword puzzle."

"I think I prefer another bad habit. Actually, bringing me crossword puzzles is getting to be a bad habit."

"This one has a title."

"What's the title?"

" 'Matt.' "

"Uh oh. Where'd you get it?"

"From his wife."

"And he doesn't know she's got it?"

"Well, he was talking to Chief Harper at the time."

"So Chief Harper doesn't know she's got it?"

"Well, I didn't want to interrupt them."

"And you're so hot to do this because it's a chance to aid a wife who's holding out on her husband?"

"And a murder suspect," Cora pointed out.

"Hasn't Chief Harper come to the conclusion she didn't do it?"

"Actually, Ratface has come to the conclusion there's not enough evidence for him to proceed with the prosecution. That doesn't mean they've given up trying."

"And how did Mrs. Greystone happen to give you this crossword puzzle?"

"When Chief Harper and I went over to see if someone was trying to kill her husband."

"What?"

Cora filled Sherry in on the automobile accident.

"So now Chief Harper thinks someone's trying to kill Matt Greystone?"

"Well, someone's clearly trying to kill someone," Cora said.

"What do you mean?"

"Matt Greystone hasn't been driving his car. When he goes out, other people drive

221

him. His wife uses the car from time to time."

"Oh?"

"Says she likes it. Since he's not going to be using it, sometimes when she goes out she takes his."

"Who knew that?"

"You have a keen detecting mind. Who knew that is certainly the question. I would imagine that is a rather select group. With Matt's agent Lenny at the top of the list."

"You think Lenny tried to kill his best client? On the surface it makes no sense."

"Any way you look at it that makes no sense. He's not going to kill his meal ticket. He may be mad at him for busting up his arm, but that would be a crazy way to show it. On the other hand, he might have a reason to get rid of Matt's wife. Only thing is, Lenny's the one who drove it off the road."

The phone rang.

Sherry snatched it off the wall, said "Hello? . . . Yeah, she's here." She held out the receiver to Cora. "Dan Finley."

Cora took the phone. "Yes, Dan?"

"I'm down at Hank Farley's garage. Hank's got Matt Greystone's car up on the lift."

"And?"

"The brake lines have been cut."

CHAPTER 37

Cora nearly beat Chief Harper there, which wouldn't have been good. The chief would have suspected Dan Finley called her first. As it was, she pulled in just behind the chief.

The car was still up on the lift.

Hank Farley came over. The station owner prided himself on his grease stains. Cora couldn't recall a time she'd seen him without one somewhere on his face. Today it was the bridge of his nose, with highlights on his left cheek.

"You say the brake lines had been cut?" Harper said.

Hank put up his hands. "Hey, I'm not the detective, I'm just the mechanic. I can show you the brake lines. I can show you the cuts halfway through. The conclusion someone made those cuts, that's your department."

"Well, can't you tell it's not a co-incidence?"

"It would be a hell of a coincidence for

them to be cut like that on both sides."

"You told Dan the lines had been cut."

"Well, sure, then it occurred to me that's your call to make. I mean, here we are, just speaking casual, I'd say, yeah, the lines have been cut. But if you're the chief of police and you're talking all official, you know, like you was gonna put me on the stand, well, I could say I found cut lines, but as to what caused 'em, that would have to be proven beyond a reasonable doubt."

Chief Harper wheeled on Cora. "Did you call Becky Baldwin?"

"Absolutely not. This man came to his position on his own. Becky's a smart lawyer, with a lot of tactics, but obfuscation isn't one of them."

"Don't you throw big words at me. It makes me think you're hiding something."

"I'm not hiding a damn thing," Cora said. "Hank Farley, you've been watching too many cop shows. I'm not a cop, I'm a private citizen, and we're just talking here together like two folks. Now, tell me what happened without tripping all over your tongue. The brakes had been cut?"

"Yeah."

"Deliberately?"

"Isn't that a legal question?"

"Yeah, but forget that for now. Let me put

it another way. Is there any way they could have been cut accidently?"

"No. Look here. See where the line's sliced halfway through and the brake fluid ran out? Same thing on the other side. You apply the brakes now and nothing's gonna happen. These lines are worthless. I gotta pull 'em out and replace 'em." He turned to Chief Harper deferentially. "When you guys say I can."

"Hold off for now. I'll give you the go-ahead. You got room to store the car?"

"I can leave it out back."

"Can you leave it inside?"

"Not while I'm working. I can roll it in at the end of the day."

"Do that for now," Harper said. "I may want someone else to see it."

"I'll have to charge something for it."

"That's fine, as long as it's reasonable."

"Now, you and I may have a different idea as to what's reasonable."

"Yeah, but we both know what's highway robbery," Harper said. "You hang on to the car. If anyone wants to see it who hasn't already been cleared, you let us know."

Harper and Cora walked out to their cars.

"You keeping the car as evidence?" Cora said.

"I wasn't going to till Hank came down

226

with a case of star witness syndrome. Could you imagine him in court? I'm going to have someone look it over who could testify if it ever came to that."

"Too bad," Cora said.

Harper frowned. "Why do you say that?"

"It would be fun laying odds on whether Hank showed up in court with grease on his face."

CHAPTER 38

Cora got back to find Jennifer racing in circles around the lawn. Buddy was gamely attempting to keep up with her. Sherry was sitting in a lawn chair watching the two of them.

"Jennifer woke up from her nap," Sherry said.

"No nap," Jennifer said as she raced by.

"Sorry," Sherry said. "Jennifer's a big girl, she doesn't take naps. The nap they weren't taking was in the playroom downstairs. Jennifer was pretending to be a sleeping dog, and Buddy was pretending to be a human and letting her lie."

"Yeah, yeah, where's the puzzle?" Cora said.

"On the kitchen table."

Cora banged through the screen door and went into the kitchen. The puzzle was in the middle of the kitchen table. Cora snatched it up, looked at it.

The puzzle was blank.

Cora's face turned red. She stomped out the front door.

"You didn't solve it."

"No."

"Why didn't you solve it?"

"I don't need to."

"Why not?"

"Did you look at it?"

"Yes, I looked at it. It's an empty grid."

"Did you look at the clues?"

"I can't solve the clues."

"Can you remember them?"

"Huh?"

"You've seen them before."

"What are you talking about?"

"It's the same puzzle you already gave me. The one that said 'Untitled.' Now it's titled."

"What?"

"It's the puzzle that said check the files. Apparently you didn't make a good job of it, so now they're telling you whose files to check."

"Are you kidding me?"

"Well, that's a conclusion on my part, but it's a pretty obvious one. Whoever created this puzzle didn't think you needed a title to figure it out. When you couldn't, they decided to give you a hint."

"Yeah, but the puzzle wasn't for me."

"Right, right, it was for Matt Greystone. Whose wife immediately gave it to you. Which was to be expected. All puzzles are basically for you."

"That's cruel, Sherry."

"I know."

"I don't understand. I already searched the witch's files. I already found the file marked 'Matt.' "

"You didn't look at it."

"I couldn't look at it, and now it's gone. Telling me to look at it is not particularly useful."

"You also found Matt's files at the gossip columnist's office."

"Yeah."

"And you looked at them. Right here on our computer. By virtue of your stolen memory card."

"Are you wearing a wire?"

"Pay attention."

"It's hard when you keep throwing out felonies you want me to casually admit to."

"The point is you got a puzzle saying check his files. You checked the witch's files. You checked Leon Bratz's computer files. You found files referring to Matt and you checked them. After that you get another copy of the puzzle telling you to check

Matt's files."

"What's your point?"

"Obviously you checked the wrong files. The puzzle maker's not going to let you get away with that. It's like the puzzle maker saying, no, idiot, you checked the wrong files."

"So?" Cora said.

Sherry cocked her head. "Didn't Leon Bratz also have a file cabinet?"

CHAPTER 39

"Well," Cora said, "this is certainly not the first time I've ever cheated on a man I was involved with, but I believe it's the first time I've ever done it with a woman."

"I'm happy to broaden your horizon," Stephanie said.

Stephanie and Cora had been friends ever since they'd met. Or at least since shortly after they first met. The meeting had been a shock to Cora, who wasn't aware that Sergeant Crowley, with whom she'd been involved, was also involved with another woman, and it had taken her awhile to adjust to the fact. Not to dealing with another woman, Cora was quite adept at that, but actually becoming acquainted with the other woman. Stephanie was the first other woman Cora had liked, and the experience was eye-opening.

It occurred to Cora the other other women she'd encountered had all been when she was still drinking, which put a different slant on it. Her tolerance when drinking was not particularly high.

"At least as far as I know I never cheated with a woman. I used to drink a lot, and I imagine the telltale signs are few. You don't wake up pregnant, for instance."

"Has that ever happened to you?"

"Not as far as I know. Of course some of the past is a bit of a blur. The seventies, for instance."

"You missed disco?"

"For the most part. I remember the Bee Gees, but that's about it."

"Can't you name another disco artist?"

"Well, if you're going to start in on the oxymorons."

Stephanie and Cora were in a taxi riding uptown from the West Village. Sergeant Crowley had come home to his Greenwich Village apartment, hoisted a few bourbons, and passed out on the couch. Stephanie had lifted his keys and met Cora at Sheridan Square. They'd planned to take the subway, but Cora was too keyed up to wait and hailed a cab.

The cab pulled up on the corner. Stephanie hopped out while Cora paid the fare.

"Okay, where is it?" Stephanie said.

"The brownstone in the middle of the block."

"They're all brownstones."

"The one with the dead man's office."

Stephanie gave Cora a look and followed her up the block to the front door of the brownstone.

"Okay, whiz kid, do your stuff."

"Hey, I just lift the keys," Stephanie said. "I don't know how to use 'em."

"Here, I'll show you," Cora said. She took the keys, held them up, and stuffed them in her drawstring purse. "You put them where they won't get in your way, and turn the doorknob."

Cora pushed the door open.

Stephanie gave her a look.

Cora smiled. "Hey, your boyfriend taught me that move. It's the next lock that's trouble."

They went up the stairs. Cora stopped in front of Leon Bratz's office door. She jerked the keys out of her purse, began rifling around the ring.

"Now, if I can remember what it looked like. Let's see. It was shaped like this." Cora tried it. "Not that one. Not this one, either. Third time's the charm? No. All right, we're eliminating possibilities."

They eliminated five more before one

turned the lock. Cora opened the door and they went in.

"Now then," Cora said, "we turn the lights on like we have every right to be here, which we certainly do. And we have a sergeant's keys to prove it."

"He will not appreciate being cited as our authorization," Stephanie said.

"If he kicks you out, I got room at my place."

"In Connecticut? I run a shop in the Village," Stephanie said.

"So let's not get caught. Okay, the computer files are worthless. We need to get into the file cabinet."

"Do we have a key that fits?"

"Sure, and the file we're looking for probably bestows immortality. The problem here is your boyfriend's seen these files. He knows what shape this cabinet was in when he wrapped the crime scene ribbon around it. He would know it had been broken into, and he would raise the alarm."

"Yes," Stephanie said, "but when he let you in here earlier — that wasn't official, was it? He didn't notify anyone, did he? He just used his keys to get in."

"You're saying he couldn't claim the file cabinet hadn't been broken into before without admitting he broke into the office?"

"Isn't that the situation?"

"I wish I brought a crowbar," Cora said.

She did pretty well with the screwdriver she found in one of Bratz's desk drawers. The decedent might have had it to hook up some of the electronic equipment in his office, but Cora had a sneaking suspicion he'd used it for mounting microphones and spy cams.

Cora made a mess of the file drawer. It occurred to her it was very much like the mess she's made of the witch's file drawer, but there was nothing she could do about that.

"All right," she said as the drawer popped open, "please, God, let the files be alphabetical."

God didn't choose to answer that prayer. Of course Cora couldn't remember the last time she'd been in church without getting married. At any rate, the files were a mess. Many of the papers weren't in folders at all. Some were in the hanging dividers that would have held folders, had Leon been that organized. The dividers were stuffed to capacity, gave the impression that papers had been stuck in willy-nilly.

Cora pulled out a bulging divider, handed it to Stephanie. "Here you go. Have a ball."

Stephanie flopped it down on the desk.

"Okay, what are we looking for?"

"Anything that might get him dead."

"That much I know."

"You're looking for any mention of Matt Greystone. That would do for a start. I have to believe he'd rate his own file. Also any mention of his wife, Jackie, who'd surely rate her own file, too."

"If she had one. You said he never printed anything about her."

"He never printed anything, but he wrote about her. It's all along the lines of 'what superstar Yankees pitcher who just signed a monster contract extension should keep better track of his wife.' "

Stephanie was already leafing through the folder.

"Also any photos that you find. I don't think he used them in his articles, and he must have had a reason for taking them."

"I haven't found any yet," Stephanie said.

"Just sayin'."

Cora continued pawing through the file drawer, looking for a likely folder. Nothing jumped out at her. She reached her hand into the cabinet, popped open the catch for the next drawer. She pulled it out and whistled.

"Find something?"

"I'll say. Our boy Leon was fond of pornography. This is his party drawer. Porn mags, a bottle of booze, and what looks like a half ounce of grass."

"Any rolling papers?"

"Stephanie, the sixties are behind us."

"Speak for yourself. I still run a tapestry shop on Bleecker Street."

"You run a high-end fabric store."

"Potato, potato," Stephanie said, pronouncing them differently. "Any files in the party drawer?"

"Yes, there are. And here's one full of photos. Featuring various men and women out on the town."

"Anyone you recognize?"

"Not offhand. Though some look vaguely familiar. Like I'd seen 'em on television for some reason or another."

"Any of them look like a psychotic killer who bumps off gossip columnists in saunas of the rich and famous?"

"The photos aren't labeled."

"Damn. That would be such a good clue."

"Don't say clue. If we come up with a crossword puzzle, I'm going to lose it."

The phone rang and Cora jumped a mile.

It was Stephanie's cell phone. She tugged it out, clicked it on. "Yeah?"

It was Sergeant Crowley. "You seen Cora?"

"Cora? No, why?"

"Her lawyer's trying to catch her. You know, Becky Baldwin."

"And she called you?"

"Relax. She's calling everyone. Cora doesn't have a cell phone. Becky's putting out the word."

"What's up?"

"Matt Greystone's wife's been arrested."

"I thought she'd already been arrested."

"She was taken in for questioning. This time she's being charged."

"They've got some new evidence?"

"Apparently they do. Becky can't find out what. That's why she needs Cora."

"If she calls me, I'll pass along the message. But she's more apt to call you."

"Where are you, anyway?"

"You passed out, so I went home."

"I didn't pass out."

"Sorry. I mean you went to sleep totally independent of the three shots of bourbon you drank. If you hadn't gotten a phone call, you'd be sleeping still. I'll see you tomorrow." Stephanie clicked the phone off.

"Wow, there's a long-term relationship," Cora said. "A lot of men wouldn't stand for that."

"Hey, what are men good for if you can't beat 'em up now and then?"

"I knew there was a reason I liked you."

"Becky's looking for you. Wanna use my phone and call her?"

"Wouldn't Crowley be able to tell I did?"

"You have a suspicious mind. Correct that, you have a devious mind that suspects men of having suspicious minds."

"Most of my men did. Of course I never had a cell phone. And few of them had the resources to access phone records. Though Melvin used to go over the monthly bills. A cop, on the other hand . . ."

"Crowley doesn't check my phone calls. We have an open relationship."

"Did you know about me before you met me?"

"Not for a while. Of course that was during an off-again period."

"Like when he was married?"

"That wasn't as off-again as it might have been," Stephanie said. "You got another file for me?"

"Anything in that one?"

"A lot of men and women. Whaddya wanna bet they aren't married to each other?"

"No takers."

"It would appear our boy Leon wasn't above a little blackmail."

"He wasn't above much," Cora said.

They leafed through the rest of the folders in the drawer without finding anything. Cora unsnapped the next one.

"Anything there?" Stephanie asked.

"We're back to straight files."

"Gimme."

Cora handed Stephanie a thick file folder. Stephanie leafed through it and whistled.

"What is it?" Cora said.

"Yet another vice. On top of his other accomplishments, Leon was a bookie."

"You're kidding."

"He's got the betting line on all the baseball games, plus who bet on 'em, how much, and whether they won or lost."

"Please tell me the name Matt Greystone isn't there."

"It's not."

"Thank goodness for small favors."

"Hey, this is good news," Stephanie said. "The motives for killing this guy are piling up."

"Yeah," Cora said. "Pete Rose, eager to get into the Hall of Fame, bumps off a bookie to hide his gambling habit."

"There you are," Stephanie said. "Reasonable doubt. Give me another file."

"Here you go."

Stephanie took the new file. She handed a stack of files to Cora. "Let's put these back, so I have room."

"Where were they from?"

"The first drawer."

Cora pulled the drawer open, but it jammed. "Hmm. Stuck on something."

"It opened before."

"Yeah, but then I opened the other drawers in a not quite kosher way. I may have shifted stuff around." Cora stuck her hand in. "Here we go. Something jammed in here."

"Can you get it free?"

"I'm trying, I'm trying."

Cora maneuvered the drawer in and out to the point of the jam. "Okay, I think we're almost there. And . . . ta-da!"

Cora pulled the offending item out of the drawer. It was a manila envelope. It wasn't sealed, but it was held closed with a metal clasp, the type with two prongs you stick through a hole and bend over. Cora undid the clasp. There was something stiff inside. She reached in, pulled it out.

It was a sheet of backing cardboard, the type you stick in an envelope to keep from crushing something.

Cora reached into the envelope to see what it had been protecting. It felt like a glossy photograph. She pulled it out.

It was.

The photograph was obviously an enlargement of a picture taken by one of Leon Bratz's spy cams. It was a picture of a young couple cozying up to each other in a singles bar.

It was Jackie Greystone and Don Upton.

CHAPTER 40

"You were having an affair with Don Up-ton?"

"Sure."

Cora choked on her tea. "What do you mean, 'sure'? That's the kind of brazen admission I used to make. And no one was happy about it. Least of all my current husband. A gossip columnist gets killed. The police are looking for a motive for you to do it. And here you are, the wife of a famous athlete, having an affair. 'Never mind the closing arguments, Your Honor, let's just march the defendant into the gas chamber.' "

"Do they have gas chambers in Con-necticut?"

"How can you joke about this? Don't you realize the trouble you're in?"

"Shouldn't I be talking to my lawyer?"

"You should. But when you do, I don't want her to have a stroke. Becky gets rather upset when clients insist on sticking their necks in the noose."

"Now you're hanging me? A minute ago you had me in the gas chamber."

Cora and Jackie were having tea on the veranda. By the time Cora got back to Bakerhaven, Jackie had been arraigned and Becky had bailed her out. Despite clawing and kicking, Becky had been unable to ascertain what new evidence the prosecution had on her client.

Becky was in no mood for another jolt. Cora had left her hanging, and gone to see Jackie.

"Did Matt know you were having an affair with Don Upton?"

"Well, I should think so. He stole me away from him."

Cora frowned. "What?"

"I was going out with Don. Who was technically married at the time." She waggled her hand. "You know how it is."

"Actually, I do," Cora said. "Wait a minute now. This was when Matt was in the minor leagues?"

"They were on the same team. Roommates, actually. Matt didn't know me. I was going out with Don. I met Matt and something clicked."

"I hate it when that happens," Cora said.

Jackie frowned. "Why?"

"In my case, it used to click too often. Never mind. You met Matt, something clicked, and Don graciously stepped aside and said, 'Take her, she's yours.' "

"It wasn't quite like that."

"No kidding. What was it like?"

"Don was very upset. To make matters worse, Matt went on a winning streak just then, and Don went on a losing one. They had a falling out, switched roommates, weren't talking to each other. Which is tough on a team. But they were starting pitchers, worked different days."

"Did you try to mend fences?"

"Oh, no. Worst thing I could have done, really. If I talked to Don, Matt would have flipped out. And if I talked to Matt about Don, that was worse."

"How come they're friends again?"

"Matt got traded. Then they were on opposite teams. Before the call-up. They got away from each other, but they had to interact. They wound up pitching against each other. I've never seen such a battle. They went nine innings, came out of the game tied zero-zero. Matt gave up three singles. Don gave up two. It got a lot of coverage for a minor league game. It was one of the reasons Matt got called up."

"Did that make for more resentment?"

"You'd think so, but it was just the opposite. It wasn't just a minor league tour anymore. Matt's with the big boys, out of town for the West Coast swing, gone for days at a time. He couldn't take me with him, but I didn't want to be left behind, and he didn't want to leave me. He had an apartment in New York. I could hang out and wait for him to get back, but that made him uneasy. The long and the short of it is we got married."

"Oh."

"Yeah. Not the most romantic of reasons, but we really cared for each other. Matt wasn't a star yet. Anyway, Don shows up at the wedding. At first I thought he was going to get drunk and make a scene, but he walks up to Matt and he grins, and he says, 'Boy, the lengths you will go to make a point.' And just like that, they were friends again."

"So, what you're saying is if Leon Bratz had a photo of you and Don together it would only be a scandal if the thing had a date stamp."

"If he did, it was Photoshopped, because Don and I haven't been out together since way back when."

"Did Leon Bratz ever try to extort you with a photo?"

"Hell, no. It wouldn't have worked if he did."

Cora sighed. "Well, that all sounds wonderful. You might try explaining it to your lawyer."

"Then what?"

"I'll try to find you another lawyer. Do you have any idea what the police have on you?"

"No."

"Yesterday they didn't have enough to charge you. Today they do. What could that be?"

"You'd have to ask them."

"Your lawyer's been doing nothing else. She's been getting no answer. Because they're on the other side. You're on her side. That's why I'm asking you."

"And I tell you I don't know."

"Did you do anything stupid between yesterday and today?"

"Like what?"

"Like whatever you did. If I knew, I wouldn't be asking. This is not a game. The disaster you've been bracing for is here. You need to take evasive action. There are various ways to do it, but holding out on your lawyer is not one of them. Where's Don?"

"He's been staying at the house."

"You didn't ask me about the crossword

puzzle."

"Oh, did you solve it?"

"I didn't have to solve it. It's the same one you got before. Only with the title filled in."

Jackie said nothing.

"You didn't know that?"

"Well, it looked like it."

"Yeah. It looked like it because it was. I'm wondering if you knew that when you gave it to me."

"Why do you say that?"

"I recall you being awfully eager for me to look at it right then and there. You were disappointed when I stuck it in my purse. Like you'd already noticed it was the same puzzle, but didn't want to admit it."

"Why would I do that?"

"That's what I was wondering."

"The point is, what do the cops think they have on me?"

"How about the fact you were having an affair with Don Upton?"

"That wouldn't bother me."

"You suppose they know that?"

"I don't know what they think. It could be the reason. I hope it is."

"Why?"

"Because it's a silly reason, and it isn't so."

"You said it was so."

"It's not a motive. It's not what the cops have on me. I wouldn't have gone out of my way to cover it up. I couldn't have cared less."

"So," Cora said, "what *do* the cops have on you?"

Jackie shrugged. "That's your job."

CHAPTER 41

"What have you got on Jackie Greystone?"

"An arrest warrant. Which I duly served."

"I know that. On the basis of what evidence?"

"She was discovered at the scene of the crime, presumably the last person to see the victim alive."

"You had all that, you let her go. Suddenly you changed your mind."

"Don't look at me. Henry Firth thought he could make a case."

"You're sparring with me, Chief."

"No fun, is it?"

"Not a good time to teach me a lesson, Chief. Becky's less than happy with the situation."

"Really? A multimillion-dollar client? Sounds like a lawyer's dream."

"Becky's not the type to pad her billable hours. She likes to get results."

"So do I."

"Then help me out. Help me to help you. You don't want to prosecute an innocent woman."

"Again, that would be Henry Firth's territory."

"You're on the prosecutor's team. So, if Ratface is so convinced she's guilty, you can let Don go."

"Huh?"

"Don Upton. He's not supposed to leave town. Now he can."

"I didn't say that."

"No, you didn't. And isn't that interesting? Could it be that Henry Firth's proceeding against both of them, but seeing as how this is a high-profile case, he's releasing the facts in dribs and drabs? I mean, why jam two arrests into one twenty-four-hour news cycle when you can stretch it out to two?"

Harper said nothing.

"Are you planning on arresting Don Upton?"

"I have no current plans."

"Would you tell me if you were?"

"I don't believe that's in my job description."

"Why in the world would Don Upton and Jackie Greystone team up to kill a penny-ante gossip columnist?"

"You tell me."

"I can't even begin to."

"Did you know they used to be an item?" Harper said.

"What makes you say that?"

"I figure you already found out by now. Particularly from the tenor of your questions."

"The tenor of my questions? Next you'll be interpreting my body language."

"Suppose he had something on them."

"I wouldn't be surprised. Leon Bratz had something on everyone."

"Suppose he could put them together."

"I'd be shocked if he couldn't. They used to date before she married Matt."

"Suppose he could put them together more recently than that."

Cora cocked her head. "Are you trying to tell me something?"

"I'm not trying to tell you something. I'm on the side of the prosecution. I'm trying to help the prosecutor build a case. I'm just saying hypothetically, for the sake of argument, suppose Leon Bratz could put them together more recently than that."

"Then I would want to know when."

"You have an inquiring mind."

"That's what Melvin said. Just before the divorce. It was one of the things that endeared me to him."

"He divorced you anyway."

"Oh, not that divorce. He said that when I was divorcing one of my other husbands. I divorced Melvin eventually, but we weren't even married then."

The phone rang.

Harper scooped it up. "Yeah? . . . Hell, be right there."

Harper slammed down the phone and lunged to his feet.

"What is it, Chief?"

"Shots fired at Matt Greystone's house."

CHAPTER 42

Harper actually used his siren. Cora couldn't remember the last time he had. He screeched to a stop and leapt out of the car. As Cora followed, there came the sound of shots from out back.

Harper raced around the side of the house, drawing his gun as he went.

Cora lost a step getting hers out of her drawstring purse. She flew around the corner and slammed into the chief, who had stopped short. He was lucky his gun didn't go off.

Matt Greystone and Don Upton were lounging by the pool in deck chairs. A dozen empty beer bottles were scattered around. They appeared to be working their way through a case. Each had a bottle of beer in one hand and a gun in the other. Don had an automatic. Matt had a revolver. They were shooting at a weathervane on the top of the sauna. It was an old-fashioned metal affair, a rooster on top of an arrow. The rooster had been nicked a few times, most likely several beers ago. As Cora watched, Don shot and missed it by a good six feet.

For Chief Harper it was a ticklish situation. Telling a drunk with a gun to put it down was an iffy proposition at best. The odds between complying with the request and shooting the requester were about equal.

Cora temporized with a hearty, "Hi, boys, got a beer?"

Matt looked up, recognized her, waved her over with his gun hand. "Come on, come on, join the party. Ah, good, you brought your gun. Come on over here. We're shooting up the vane." He broke off, frowned. "That sounds bad. Shooting up the vane. I don't mean we're intravenous drug users. We're shooting up the weathervane. Hit the rooster, win a beer."

"What if I miss the rooster?" Cora said.

"You win a beer. Okay, my turn, my turn."

"No way," Cora said. "You had your turn. It's my turn. Put your guns down. Put your guns down. That's it. Right there."

Chief Harper came up behind them and scooped up the guns from the end tables. "All right, boys, what's going on?"

Don looked up. "It's a game, Chief." His

eyes widened. "A policeman. Hey, Matt, it's the cops. Act natural."

"Okay."

Matt took acting natural to mean holding himself rigid and not looking in any direction. He frowned. "Why are we hiding from the cops?"

"We're not hiding from the cops. We're acting natural."

"Okay." Matt's face clouded. "Whose shot is it?"

"Where's your wife, Matt?" Chief Harper said.

"Where *is* my wife?" Matt said. "That is the question. I think she got arrested. That's right. She got arrested, and we're gonna bust her out of jail. Just as soon as we get good enough. We're practicing up, and then we're going to bust her out of jail."

"She's out of jail," Harper said.

"It worked!" Matt cried happily. He leapt from his chair, teetered on unsteady feet, and plunged headfirst into the pool.

Luckily Don was sober enough to pull him out, otherwise it would have fallen upon Chief Harper or Cora, fully dressed and holding a gun, to make the sacrifice. Just working out the logistics probably would have taken long enough to let the Yankee star pitcher drown. But Don managed to push him close enough to the edge of the pool for Cora and Chief Harper to haul him up. They wrestled him into a lounge chair and put in a call to his wife.

Matt couldn't remember her number, and Don either couldn't remember or didn't want to show off the fact he could remember in front of Matt, which would have required far more cognitive thought than he appeared capable of in his inebriated condition, so Harper called Becky Baldwin, who hadn't heard from her.

Cora had a sudden premonition that if she were to pull open the sauna door she would find Jackie Greystone's bullet-ridden body, but that seemed like something out of a mystery novel and way beyond the realm of possibility. Nonetheless, she left Chief Harper in charge of the two drunks, and trudged over to the sauna with mounting dread.

The crime scene ribbon was still up. It was hanging loosely enough that a determined snoop could get the door open wide enough to slip in. Cora didn't bother to enter. She merely pulled the door open and looked.

The sauna was empty.

Cora heaved a huge sigh of relief and went back to the pool, where Chief Harper was advising the two young gunslingers on why they might not want to call out for pizza.

There came the sound of a car stopping in front of the house.

"The pizza!" Matt cried, struggling to get out of his chair.

"Relax," Don said. "They deliver."

Matt's agent bustled around the side of the house. He took one look, said, "Oh, my God!"

"It's all right," Cora said. "We disarmed them."

"You what!"

"We took their guns."

"Where'd you get ahold of a gun?" Lenny demanded.

"Wasn't easy," Matt said. "Someone hid our guns. But we had a scavenger hunt."

"Yeah," Don said. "We had a scavenger hunt and we found a gun. Then we had a gun hunt and we found a scavenger."

The agent was white as a sheet. "They could have killed themselves!"

"That seems entirely likely," Cora said. "But Matt just fell in the pool."

"He fell in the pool!"

"Yeah, but Don jumped in and held his head out of the water until we pulled him up."

"You pulled him up? By his bad arm?"

That hadn't even occurred to Cora. But if they'd hurt his arm, he probably wouldn't have noticed.

"Where's Jackie?"

"She isn't here," Harper said. "We just responded to a report of shots fired."

"Someone filed a report? Who was it? I've gotta talk to them."

"I don't know who filed the report. Even if I did, talking to them would not be advisable. It might lead to complications."

"I don't see why. No one's filing any charges, are they?"

"Rookie mistake," Cora said. "Never be the first one to mention filing charges. If you were a lawyer, you'd know that."

Lenny might not have heard her. "What were they shooting?" he said to Chief Harper.

"The sauna."

"Before you freak out, I looked inside and there's no bullet-ridden body," Cora said. "At the moment they were thinking of sending out for pizza."

"Oh, my God!"

"You're concerned about publicity?"

"Of course."

"Then you better think fast. That looks like the Channel 8 news van heading up the road."

Lenny spotted the van, turned on Chief Harper. "They can't do that. You chased them away."

"I did. But this is something new. Report of shots fired. It's breaking news. Of course they can cover it."

"Oh, my God! Get inside, get inside, get inside!"

Don looked up. "Who's the spoilsport?"

"That's my agent," Matt said. "He's trying to get me a commercial."

"A beer commercial? Hey, Lenny, how about a beer commercial?"

"We gotta clean up. Everybody grab beer bottles. Not you guys. You gotta go inside. The news crew can't see this. They can't come out back, can they?"

"I wouldn't expect them to stand on ceremony," Cora said.

"Clean up, clean up!"

"Yeah," Harper said. "I don't really want the news team to find me cleaning up the scene of a drunken debauch."

Lenny had managed to herd the two pitchers into the house, but as he came back to deal with the beer bottles, they wandered back with him. He gave it up as a lost cause, turned, and fled around the house.

"Think he'll be able to stop Rick Reed?" Harper said.

"Probably not, but it might be fun to watch."

Cora followed Chief Harper around the side of the house. Looking back over her shoulder, she saw Matt opening up another beer.

Rick Reed's camera crew was already filming.

"We hear there's been trouble," Rick said. "Where's Matt Greystone?"

"You've been misinformed," Lenny said. "There's no trouble. Matt Greystone is fine. He's rehabbing from an injury, and needs his privacy."

"There's been the report of a disturbance. Shots fired."

"Where did you hear that?" Lenny said.

Rick Reed was taken aback. "There was a report."

"To you?"

"To me? No, not to me."

"Then I cannot comment on an unsubstantiated report that has been proven wrong."

"I take it back," Cora said. "You might make a good lawyer."

A scream from in back of the house froze them in their tracks. It was a woman's scream, loud, blood-curdling. In an instant the standoff with the news crew was forgotten, as everyone raced around the house.

Matt and Don were gone, but there was not a chance they'd gone inside. Branches could be heard snapping in the woods. Chief Harper and Cora ran around the pool, guns drawn, ready for anything.

There came a jumble of raised voices.

Matt's anguished scream cut through all of them. "Noooo!"

A cold chill ran down Cora's spine. She stumbled, nearly crashed into a tree. She cursed, righted herself, kept going.

Cora burst into the clearing. The first thing she saw was the camera. Rick Reed had sent an auxiliary unit out back in the hope of sneaking shots of the pool. They were clearly the B-team, a man and woman so young Cora might have mistaken them for a college movie crew had the camera not had a Channel 8 logo.

It was the young woman who had screamed. Now she was making up for it by barking terse orders at the cameraman. She seemed torn between letting the camera cover the scene, and jumping in with a microphone.

Matt Greystone looked stricken. He was leaning against a tree trunk. It seemed to be taking what was left of his wits just to retain his balance.

Don stood regarding the scene. He had his head cocked to one side, and a somewhat bemused expression on his face, as if he'd ordered another round of beer and instead he'd gotten this.

A woman's body lay in the dirt. Her face and hair were smeared with mulch, dried leaves, and blood. She'd been shot. Her eyes were open, glassy, staring. She was clearly dead.

Lenny burst into the clearing. He took in the scene. He looked as if his entire life had just flashed before his eyes. "Matt?"

Matt Greystone raised his eyes.

Jackie Greystone appeared out of nowhere and flung herself into his arms. In his inebriated state she almost knocked him down, but he clung to her, and the two of them stood there, swaying, holding each other.

Cora looked back at the body on the ground.

The hair, which looked brown covered with dirt and leaves, was actually red.

It wasn't Jackie Greystone.

It was the witch.

CHAPTER 43

This time the TV crews wouldn't leave.
They were camped outside the police station, and there were more arriving every
minute. This time it was national news, not
just local news that gets picked up on the
national evening broadcast, but breaking
news, the lead story on every twenty-four-
hour news network. This was not just an
anomaly being reported because it had
taken place at a celebrity's barbecue. This
was OJ in the Bronco.

All things considered, Becky Baldwin was
holding together remarkably well. It
couldn't have been easy. She had two
clients, both of whom looked guilty, and
one of whom was still incredibly drunk. Yet
she managed to appear as calm as if she
were reporting on the PTA luncheon as she
fielded a barrage of questions.

"Ms. Baldwin. Are you representing Matt
Greystone or Jackie Greystone?"

"I'm representing both of them."

"Isn't that a conflict of interest?"

"Not at all. Their interests are the same."

"Is that true?" Cora said, after she and Becky escaped into the police station.

"Is what true?" Becky said.

"That their interests are the same?"

"I wouldn't go that far," Becky said. "But we have two separate crimes, the murder of Leon Bratz and the murder of Amanda Hoyt. It's entirely possible he killed one and she killed the other."

"How can you say that? You're their attorney."

"That's how I can say that. You're not going to quote me, are you?"

"You know what would be neat?" Cora said.

"What?"

"If the police charged the wrong one."

Becky frowned. "What?"

"Well, if they charged Jackie with killing Leon Bratz, and she's innocent because he did it, and they charge Matt with killing the witch, and he's innocent because she did it."

"I fail to see how that helps me."

"You see exactly how that helps you. You just don't want to admit it because you're a lawyer."

"You're saying the fact they prosecuted the wrong one means they can't get a conviction. Not that *I* would prove one didn't do it because the other did."

"Exactly."

"And I would just keep quiet and allow these murderers to go free."

"While you deposit their checks, let's not forget that."

"I know you're joking, Cora, but do you have the slightest suspicion that happened?"

"I don't have the slightest idea *what* happened."

The doctor came in the front door.

"Ah, here's Barney Nathan. Let's see what he can do about getting your client out of here."

Matt Greystone was asleep on a cot in the lockup in the back of the police station. Chief Harper had done Becky Baldwin the favor of taking him in on a charge of drunk and disorderly, a charge that would be dropped before arraignment, but that while in effect would allow the young man to escape from the media.

It went without saying that having him in jail would be convenient if the police should decide to proceed against him in the death of Amanda Hoyt.

"Chief, Barney's here to examine the prisoner."

"Be my guest," Harper said. "He's out back."

"I'll have to get into the cell," Barney said.

"Oh, of course. Dan."

Dan Finley, who was sorry to have missed out on the second homicide, was eager to pick up what he could from eavesdropping.

Barney, Cora, and Becky followed Dan Finley to the holding cells out back.

Matt Greystone was snoring noisily on the narrow cot in his cell. Dan Finley unlocked the door.

Don was sitting up in the adjoining cell. "That's right, that's right," he said. "Check on the star. Give him medical attention. Never mind the minor leaguer. Let him die, for all you care."

Barney Nathan went into Matt's cell. He opened his doctor's bag, put on his stethoscope, and listened to Matt's chest.

Barney recoiled from the pitcher's breath. "Whoa! You don't have to be a doctor to pronounce this man drunk."

"How's his arm?" Cora said. "He's lying on it kind of funny."

Barney tried to untangle Matt's arm. Matt flinched and pulled away.

"It bothers him."

"Of course it bothers him. That's a million bucks a start he's not getting. That would bother anyone."

Matt's agent pushed his way in. "How about it, doc? He's in no shape to face the media. You probably just want to knock him out with a sedative and send him to bed."

Barney Nathan adjusted his red bow tie, stuck his nose in the air, and cleared his throat.

"Barney usually likes to make his own diagnosis," Becky said. "But I'm sure he'll keep that in mind."

"You stay out of it," Chief Harper said to Lenny.

"All right," Barney said. "He's in no shape to talk to anyone. I could move him to the hospital, but then you'd have to post a twenty-four-hour guard."

"And the media will report that you did, and be waiting there when he gets out," Lenny said.

"Oh, I think I can handle that," Barney said. He walked out of the room, jerking his cell phone from his pocket. He was back minutes later. "All right," he said. "Let's go meet the media."

With Barney Nathan marching ahead, they all trouped out the front door of the police station.

The TV reporters were waiting to pounce.

"Dr. Nathan, were you brought in to examine Matt Greystone?"

"Yes, I was."

"And what did you find?"

"Mr. Greystone is in no shape to answer questions. He has received a severe shock as a result of having a second violent crime take place on his premises. He finds this overwhelming. This is not surprising. Anyone would. Being exposed to questioning at this time could only result in trauma. As a doctor, I absolutely forbid it. I have ordered bed rest, and I am going to see that's what he gets."

"Is it true he's being held in custody?"

"That's not my department. I was called upon to examine him in my capacity as a doctor. Questions of that nature are better addressed to other people. I can only speak as to his physical condition with regard to answering questions. And I intend to see that my patient is left alone."

An ambulance with flashing lights came down the street, turned into the side alley, and drove around to the back of the station.

"Hey, what's with the ambulance, Doc?"

"Is that for Matt Greystone?"

"Did you order that?"

"I'm glad you asked me that," Barney

270

Nathan said. "It gives me a chance to clear up a few things. Now, pay close attention because —"

But the news crews had already caught the scent and were following the ambulance into the alley.

There came the sound of a siren and the flashing of lights, and newsmen jumped for cover as the ambulance hurtled out of the alley and sped off in the direction of the hospital.

The news crews ran for their vans and took off in hot pursuit.

"They're going to catch up!" Lenny said.

"Oh, I doubt that," Barney said.

"They'll film him checking in! It will be a disaster! It's not enough he's a murder suspect, he'll come off like an idiot!"

"I certainly hope not," Barney Nathan said. "You better get over there to make sure that doesn't happen."

Lenny gave him a look, then ran across the street and took off in his car.

"You going to meet them at the hospital, Barney?" Chief Harper said.

The doctor smiled, snapped his red bow tie. "No, I think I'll go home and have a drink. My job here is done."

"What!"

"Well, almost done. I have to check on

271

one thing."

The doctor went back into the police station. Cora, Becky, Dan, and the chief tagged along after him. Dr. Nathan walked through the outer office and made his way down the back hallway to the holding cells.

Don Upton was still sitting on his cot.

Matt Greystone was passed out on his.

"Ah, excellent," Barney said. "The patient is asleep, my work is done. I think I'll have that drink."

He grinned, turned on his heel, and walked out.

Cora's face cracked into a smile. "I'll be damned!" she whispered.

Chief Harper turned to her. "Are you telling me he did that for you?"

"Don't be silly," Cora scoffed. "Barney still crosses the street when he sees me coming. Trust me, he wouldn't do anything for me."

"So, what's so funny?"

"I just figured it out."

"What's that?"

Cora grinned. "He's a Yankee fan."

CHAPTER 44

"Let's get back to the office," Becky said.

"Why?"

"I stashed Jackie Greystone there."

"In your office? She must be going nuts."

"It's a nice office."

"Not when your husband's in jail and you might be next. It's a place to pace the room and wonder what's going on. And there's not much room to pace."

"Better than a big, empty house that's a crime scene with cops and reporters stumbling around."

"Well, when you put it that way."

Becky unlocked the office door.

Jackie Greystone sprang from her chair. "Did you get him out?"

"I left him in," Becky said.

"What?"

"Reporters think he's in the hospital. Actually, he's sleeping it off in a cell."

"What about Don?"

"Same thing, but he's not as drunk."

Jackie nodded. "Matt never could hold his liquor. So, how'd you manage that?"

"The doctor helped us pull it off. He's a Yankees fan. Lenny went to the hospital to help sell the idea."

"That's nice of him."

"Just prudent. He's making sure no one films Matt in his current condition."

The news crews were desperate for footage. The cops had impounded all footage at the crime scene as evidence. Money shots of Matt in anguish were in custody.

"We gotta talk turkey," Becky said. "Anything you tell me in front of Cora is not privileged. So if you're going to say anything incriminating, I'll send her away."

"I've done nothing. Neither has Matt."

"If you say so."

"I do. We'll get along a lot better if you believe me."

"I believe you. And I want to trust you. But there's some things that don't add up."

"Like what?"

"Amanda Hoyt was at the party."

"So?"

"Was she on the guest list?"

"No, she wasn't."

"Did you invite her?"

"No."

"Did Matt?"

"No, of course not."

"Then why was she there?"

Jackie shrugged. "She wanted to go."

"They were checking invitations at the gate."

"She got in."

"You blame the batboy?"

"Not at all. I'm sure he did a fine job. But if people want to get in, they're going to get in. It's not like the property is fenced."

"At any rate, she got in."

"Yes."

"Why would she have come back?"

"I have no idea."

Cora gave a short, pungent exclamation of disbelief.

"You doubt my word?"

"Save the indignant act. You gave me a crossword puzzle that when solved said check the file. The witch's files were broken into. One file she was particularly concerned with and wanted the police to check for fingerprints, was alphabetically right where Greystone would be."

"That doesn't prove anything."

"No, but when I didn't find the file, I got another puzzle helpfully titled 'Matt.' And, guess what? It's the same puzzle. Check the file. Whose file? Matt's file. I can understand why Matt wouldn't want people thinking he believed in the occult. He'd be laughed off the mound. Except now it's a murder and no one's laughing. If he was seeing the woman professionally, the cops are going to find out. It's going to look like she had something on him and Matt killed her to cover it up."

"Now Matt's the killer?" Jackie said. "I thought the police charged me."

"They're flexible," Cora said.

"The theory is Matt killed her for the same reason he killed Leon Bratz?"

"Of course."

"Matt was nowhere near the sauna."

"No, but you were. If you and Matt were in this together."

"Were in what together?"

"I don't know," Cora said. "That's just one theory. Here's another. When I burst into the clearing, I thought it was you on the ground. Not that she looked like you. I thought that from Matt's reaction. But Matt knew it wasn't you. He'd been there. He'd seen the body. And yet he reacted as if he'd lost the love of his life. Is it possible that Matt and Amanda Hoyt were having an affair?"

"Don't be absurd."

"Why is that absurd? She was a good-looking woman."

"She was twice his age."

Cora smiled as if the comment hadn't gone through her like a knife. The witch, whose youth she'd envied, was twice Matt's age. The realization she wasn't, it was just an expression, didn't make it any better. "I don't think you can expect the prosecutor to accept a difference in ages as a bar to intimacy."

"This is silly. I want to get home."

"You probably don't," Becky said.

Jackie looked at her. "What?"

"There are reporters at the house. They'll be staking out the place. They'll want to ask you questions."

"I don't have to answer."

"No, you don't. But they'll get footage of you going by and not answering questions. You know what they'll play it over? A commentary speculating on where your husband is. All your going home will do is play up the fact Matt isn't there. All the media's got right now is speculation over the fact he's checked into a hospital. Which is going to make them look pretty silly tomorrow when they're forced to take it back."

"It's a very neat thing your lawyer has maneuvered for you," Cora said. "She's virtually done the impossible. Taken a publicity crisis, and manipulated it to your advantage. It's much better to sit tight and let them speculate."

"All right," Jackie said. "But if I can't go home, and I can't stay here, where am I going to go?"

Cora smiled. "Be my guest."

CHAPTER 45

Jennifer was delighted to have company. She was certain Jackie Greystone had come just to see her. Luckily, Jackie was charmed rather than annoyed, and was willing to tag along as Jennifer showed her the house.

"I know I should have called," Cora said.

"It's all right," Sherry told her.

"It would have been awkward. She'd have seen I had to ask, and automatically said no."

"I understand."

"Aaron's out chasing the story?"

"He called from the hospital."

"Tell him to come home."

"He can report that Jackie Greystone's staying here?"

"No, but he's better off here than there."

"Do I want to know why?"

"Probably not."

"So, what do the police have on the victim?" Sherry said.

"On the victim? Not on the crime?"

"If they had anything on the crime you'd have led with it. I'm assuming the ballistics report hasn't come back?"

"If it has, they're not telling us."

"If the bullet was from Matt Greystone's gun they'd be telling us. Of course, there's two guns involved. Do the police know who was firing which?"

"As a matter of fact, I don't think they do."

"Interesting."

"You've given this a lot of thought."

"Well, Jennifer and I went to the movies. My mind wanders during children's movies."

"What did you see?"

"I have no idea."

"So you thought about guns."

"And the victim," Sherry said. "Have the police made any progress with the victim?"

"What do you mean?"

"Well, it's interesting. First she's the victim of a robbery. Now she's the victim of a murder. She's either very unlucky or the crimes are connected."

"Yeah," Cora said, "and whaddya want to bet the connection is Matt Greystone? Since there was all that commotion about his file."

"The witch didn't have his file."

"The witch didn't *produce* his file. She produced the folder that could have *held* his file."

"What I don't understand," Sherry said, "is why she had the files at her house to begin with."

"What do you mean?"

"Wouldn't it make more sense to keep them at her office?"

"They were in her office."

"Not her home office. Her office in the City. She has a business office on Sixth Avenue. Why wouldn't her files be there?"

"The witch has an office on Sixth Avenue?"

"Sure."

"Where did you hear this? Was it on the news?"

Sherry shook her head. "I don't think they have it yet. I just Googled her, and that's what I got."

Cora's mouth fell open. "She has an office in the City and no one knows about it?"

CHAPTER 46

"This is getting to be a bad habit," Stephanie said.

"You love it and you know it," Cora said as she leafed through Sergeant Crowley's key ring.

The downstairs door of the witch's office building was somewhat more formidable than that of Leon Bratz. It was taking too long for comfort. Cora had just managed to fit a key into the lock only to discover it wouldn't turn, when a woman got off the elevator and headed for the door.

The lobby was small, the distance was short, and Cora was caught red-handed.

The woman held the door open for them and smiled. "Your key sticks, too? I have so much trouble with that door."

"Some days you get lucky," Cora said as they rode up in the elevator.

"And how," Stephanie said. "Crowley would not have been amused bailing us out, particularly when he saw his keys."

"He might not have seen them," Cora said. "They'd have been in the envelope with all our possessions they took away before they put us in the holding cell."

"What holding cell? You've been living in the sticks too long. They'd have thrown us in the drunk tank."

"I hate it when that happens."

"You've been there before?"

"Probably. When you're drinking, who remembers?"

The witch's office had a plain wooden door with no nameplate.

"You sure this is it?" Stephanie said.

"According to Sherry. I'd take her word on anything."

"You trust yourself to translate it correctly?"

"I wrote it down." Cora took out the keys, started on the lock. "Of course she's just going by what she found on Google."

"Now you tell me."

"Relax. How mad could Crowley be?"

"If he caught us with his keys we might have to calm him down with a threesome."

Cora dropped the keys on the floor. She stooped, picked them up. "Now you sound like Melvin."

"He was your husband?"

"Not at the time."

A key turned in the lock.

"See? Easy," Cora said. "Now we just push it open and the alarm goes off."

"Bite your tongue."

There was no alarm. They went in, locked the door behind them, and switched on the lights.

The witch had a small waiting room with two chairs and a table with back-dated magazines.

The inner office had a desk with a computer, a swivel chair, a couple of client's chairs, and a metal file cabinet.

"That's not going to open," Stephanie said.

Cora pulled a pry bar out of her drawstring purse. "I beg to differ."

"You can't pry that open."

"Why not?"

"You'll taint the investigation. The police will think the killer did it."

"I doubt if that will make any difference in whether they solve the crime."

"I see what you're doing," Stephanie said. "You want me to get caught, so Crowley will think I'm as bad as you."

"Nonsense. No one's as bad as me."

"Let's see what's on the computer. Maybe we won't have to open the file."

"It's probably password protected."

It wasn't.

Cora clicked the mouse and the computer roared to life. The screen was filled with icons, many of them helpfully labeled something meaningless in most societies.

Icons from the major programs were in a bar along the bottom.

"Ah, Quicken," Cora said. "What are the odds?"

The odds were not good. Quicken was password protected, and the obvious passwords like "password," "1234," and the woman's name failed to open it.

Cora opened the woman's email and did a search for the name Greystone. She was relieved when it didn't come up.

One icon had the day's date. Cora clicked on it and a calendar appeared. "Here we go."

Stephanie looked over her shoulder. "What is it?"

"It looks like her appointment book. There's a calendar with appointments filled in. Tomorrow she had four of them. Eleven, twelve, two, and four. With names after them. Jameson, B. Maxwell, F. Carson, D. And Cohen, R. I guess those are clients."

"They're going to be disappointed," Stephanie said. "Does it scroll back any?"

"I'll bet it does."

There came a sound from the outer office.

Cora closed the calendar, leapt up from the chair.

An old man came in with a set of keys and a gun. He didn't seem comfortable with the gun, probably hadn't pulled it in all his years on the job.

"Hands up!" he ordered. His voice cracked, and his hand shook.

Cora was sure he'd accidently shoot them.

"Yes, of course," she said. "This is our fault. We should have informed you before we went in. But Amanda Hoyt is dead. She was murdered in the town where she lived, Bakerhaven, Connecticut. I'm from Bakerhaven. I'm the Puzzle Lady, and I often assist the police in matters of this type. If you'd be so good as to not aim that gun at me, I'm sure we could straighten all this out."

The guard kept hold of his gun. Having finally had cause to draw it, he wasn't about to put it away. "If the woman's dead, no one's got a right to be in here. Except the police."

"You called the police."

"Damn right I did. So let's everybody hang on until the police get here and take charge. How's that sound?"

Stephanie shot Cora a look.

"Couldn't be better," Cora said.

CHAPTER 47

Crowley could not have looked more embarrassed had he been bailing two hookers out of jail. He managed not to explode until he got Cora and Stephanie out to his car.

"What the hell were you thinking?" he thundered.

"I'm glad you asked that," Cora said. "This is horribly confusing, and I'd love to run a few theories by you."

"Tell me you didn't get arrested just to run a few theories by me."

"No, that was just a by-product."

"Cora, I don't think he appreciates your humor," Stephanie said.

"And you," Crowley said. "I mean, I expect this sort of thing out of her, but you used to have sense. At least for a peace/love hippie chick. I could count on you to act rationally. Then you meet Cora, and suddenly all that goes out the window."

"Since you met Cora, *you've* been rational

as ever."

"I haven't been arrested breaking into any offices."

"It's not that you haven't broken into them. It's because you're a cop."

"Don't you want to know what we found?" Cora said.

"No, I don't want to know what you found with your illegal search," Crowley said. "Whatever it is, it's now tainted and can't be used in court."

"Court, schmort," Cora said. "I'm not talking about evidence. I'm talking about leads. And don't give me any fruit of the poisonous tree nonsense. I'm talking about private knowledge that can point a police officer in the right direction."

After a pause Crowley said, "Which is?"

Victory. For Cora, after a lifetime of manipulating half a dozen or so husbands, it was nothing to write home about, still anything that took the heat off of Stephanie would be a help.

"When we were apprehended, I'd just found the woman's appointment calendar."

"Appointment calendar?"

"That's right. With the names of the chumps she'd managed to hoodwink into seeing her."

"Anyone interesting?"

"I don't know," Cora said. "I was about to look when Mike Hammer burst in with his gun drawn and arrested us."

"And there's your fruit of the poisonous tree," Crowley said. "If we find the name of the killer in her files, we won't be able to use it."

"If you find the name of the killer in the files, I imagine there'll be enough evidence against him or her you won't need it."

"Or her? Are you implying his wife did it?"

"Certainly not. I'm merely using a nonsexist designation to identify the killer so that female murderers won't feel slighted."

"Isn't it murderesses?" Stephanie said.

"You're not kidding me out of it," Crowley said. "This is unacceptable and this has to stop. I'd really hate to think you were a bad influence on Stephanie."

"Is that how we rank in your estimation?" Cora said. "She's a good girl and I'm bad news?"

"Oh, no," Crowley said. "You're not making me the bad guy in all this. Let's not forget how we got here. You got caught breaking and entering."

"And you galloped in on your white horse and saved us," Cora said. "Now, if we could discuss this without recriminations, we

290

might get a little further. The woman had appointments. Wouldn't it be interesting to find out if she was seeing anyone we know?"

"It certainly would," Crowley said. "And I'm sure that is one of the things the police will look into."

"You're the police."

"The police investigating the crime. I'm the New York police. I'm not investigating crimes in Connecticut."

"Last I looked, this was New York City," Cora said.

"You want me to investigate your breaking and entering? I'm sure I can find evidence of your guilt, but that might be a conflict of interest since I just put up your bail. I'm dropping you at your car. Then I have a hot date with a bottle of Jack Daniel's, and I'll see if I have the slightest chance of ever getting back to sleep."

CHAPTER 48

Stephanie couldn't believe Cora was calling. "You gotta be kidding."

"I'm not."

"It's idiotic."

"No, it's perfect."

"We got caught stealing his keys."

"Exactly. He caught us once, he'll never expect us to do it again."

"Yeah, because it would be stupid. We put him on his guard."

"To do what? Lock his keys in a safe-deposit vault? I don't think that's his style. Besides, it's not like we're breaking into the witch's office. That he's been alerted to. We'll be breaking into the gossip columnist's office."

"Which we've also broken into."

"Yeah, but he doesn't know it. We didn't get caught. No officious watchman with a shaky gun hand came around."

"I thought he was going to shoot us."

292

"It seemed quite likely. He might have hit the trigger by accident. But this is an entirely different office building. He doesn't work there. The gods of Dork will not have miraculously transferred him from where we were to where we're going."

"We're not going."

"Not unless you get those keys. It would be a hard door to get in without them. I might have to resort to my feminine wiles."

"You have feminine wiles?"

"You'd better believe it."

"That could get you in the door?"

"That's nothing compared to other things they've got me."

"I don't think I want to know."

"Did Crowley hear the phone?"

"Crowley's sound asleep."

"There you are. We'll be back before he knows it."

"So, what are you looking for?"

"A man who doesn't break my heart."

"I mean realistically."

"Um, catty, I like that."

"Seriously. What are you really looking for? I mean, you searched the office. What are you looking for this time?"

"Meet you there," Cora said, and hung up the phone.

CHAPTER 49

Stephanie was there. She didn't look happy, but she had Crowley's keys.

"All right, what's the big idea?" she said. "Why are we here?"

"I don't want to overlook the obvious."

"What's the obvious?"

"Leon Bratz was a sleaze."

"I don't think we overlooked that."

"Yes, and no. We know Leon Bratz is a sleaze. We take it as a given. When we find him doing anything sleazy we take it for granted. It doesn't raise any red flags."

"So?"

"I have an idea. I hope I'm wrong."

"About what?"

Cora clicked the door open, switched the light on. "It doesn't look like anyone's been here since last time."

"If they have, they didn't fix the file cabinet. Please don't get us caught again."

"Wouldn't dream of it."

Cora walked over to the file cabinet, jerked open Leon Bratz's party drawer with the liquor and the skin mags. She picked up a pile of magazines and handed them to Stephanie. "Here you go. Let's read some porn."

"What are we looking for?"

"Anything that jumps out at you."

Stephanie sat down and started leafing through the magazines.

"Learning any new positions?" Cora said.

"These aren't hard-core. Just skin mags."

"Life is full of disappointments."

Cora flipped a page and stopped dead.

She was looking at a shot of Jackie Greystone.

CHAPTER 50

Becky Baldwin rubbed the sleep out of her eyes. "This better be good."

"That depends on your definition of good."

"Cora."

"I got arrested."

"For what?"

"Breaking and entering."

"What did you do now?"

"I broke into the witch's office."

"I thought you did that already."

"Not her office here. Her office in the City."

"She had an office in the City?"

"Right. The witch had an office in the City, and the police didn't know about it."

"Until you got arrested."

"Yeah, but it's the New York police. It will take time for it to filter down."

"Will it filter down?"

"Crowley will probably call Chief Harper."

"Crowley arrested you?"

"No, he bailed us out."

"Us?"

"Stephanie was with me."

"Crowley must have loved that."

"You wouldn't have known from his body language."

"I'll bet. Okay, what's the good news?"

"That *is* the good news."

"You're kidding."

"No."

"How is that good news?"

"We know that the witch had an apartment in the City. It's where she kept her appointments. She had four or five a day. They're listed on her computer in an appointment calendar. The times and the names."

"Anyone we know?"

"I got arrested before I could look."

"Damn. And that's the bad news?"

"No."

"What's the bad news?"

"I did it again."

"What?"

"Breaking and entering."

"And got the names?"

"No."

"Why not?"

"I didn't break into the witch's office. That would be suicide. The police would be sure to have it sewn up."

"Cora, I'm half asleep. What the hell did you do?"

"I broke into Leon Bratz's office. I was afraid he had something on your client. Turns out I was right."

"Which client?"

"The pretty one who doesn't pitch."

"Right now that's either of them."

"Damned if it isn't. The young lady. Jackie Greystone. Turns out he had something on her."

"What's that?"

"Naked pictures."

CHAPTER 51

Jackie Greystone was sleeping in the room next to Cora's. It was the room that used to be Sherry's before she married Aaron and moved into the new addition. Jackie was sleeping rather peacefully for a woman who had had two murders on her property and whose husband was in jail.

Cora shook her awake. "Get up, get up, time's a wasting."

Jackie opened her eyes to find Cora and Becky looking down at her. "What the hell?"

"Wake up. It's another day, and another trauma."

"Matt?"

"Matt's fine. At least I assume Matt's fine. I haven't seen him in a while, but I would say he's a damn sight better than you."

"What do you mean?"

"Leon Bratz had naked pictures of you."

Jackie Greystone raised her eyebrows. "I beg your pardon?"

"He had pictures of you in a girlie mag. You don't look bad."

"What in the world are you talking about?"

"Leon Bratz. The man who was killed on your estate in your sauna. The man you walked in on and found dead. He had pictures of you naked. Can I assume you knew that?"

"You can assume anything you like. It won't make it true."

"Hold on a minute," Becky said. "You didn't know he had the pictures?"

"I didn't know a thing about Leon Bratz except he was a pain in the ass gossip columnist. When I found him dead I wasn't sorry."

"That's probably not a good thing for you to spread around."

"Yes, yes, all God's creatures and all that. Leon Bratz was one of those parasites who write those snide articles insinuating all kinds of things. It's hard to feel bad about someone like that."

"You don't need to feel bad," Becky said, "but it's probably better not to glory in his death."

"We're getting off subject," Cora said. "We were talking about naked pictures. You mind telling me how they wound up in a girlie mag?"

"Clearly someone pointed a camera and took a picture."

"Did you pose for the pictures?"

"Do they look posed?"

"Yes."

"Then they probably are."

"You're taking this awfully casually."

"This is not a big deal in this day and age."

"It is when the guy with the pictures is a gossip columnist you found dead."

"I can see how that would look bad."

"Does Matt know about the pictures?"

"I don't know. He never mentioned it."

"You didn't volunteer the information?"

"The subject never came up."

"You never mentioned it?"

"No. Did you tell your husbands everything you ever did?"

"Not even in court," Cora said. "But you can tell me. Did you know Leon Bratz had naked pictures of you?"

"I don't even know now. I only have your word for it."

"Trust me, he had 'em. Was he holding them over your head?"

"This is the first I've heard of it. So, you found some pictures. I trust you destroyed them. And how do I know you're not making it up?"

"It's not the sort of thing I'd do."

Becky coughed discreetly.

"All right, it *is* the sort of thing I'd do," Cora said. "No, I did not destroy the pictures. Becky and I are a full service operation, but we draw the line at actually committing crimes."

Becky coughed again.

"Would you stop doing that?" Cora said irritably. "I'm trying to paint us in the best possible light. Right now that isn't particularly rosy."

"You got any more surprises you'd like to drop on my client while she's half asleep and vulnerable?"

"What about the theory Matt and the woman were having a fling?"

"I told you they weren't."

"Yeah, but now that you've had some time to think about it."

"There's no connection."

"Yeah, there is, and the cops are going to find it."

Jackie took a breath. "All right, who knows about this?"

"The three of us, and my friend, Stephanie."

"Will she tell anyone?"

"No. Well, maybe her boyfriend."

"Who's her boyfriend?"

"Sergeant Crowley."

"A *cop*?"

"When you say it like that it sounds bad."

"If you were trying to shock me awake, you've done it. This woman is going to tell her boyfriend, who's a cop. Who's going to tell the other cops, and then I'll get arrested."

"You've already been arrested."

"All right. Let's go talk to Matt."

"We can't do that."

"Why not?"

"There's reporters in town. They think he's in the hospital, but they can't get in to see him. If you show up at the jail, they'll know he's there."

"You mean he can't get out?"

"I didn't say that."

CHAPTER 52

The two men who came to fix the air conditioner were a moral victory for Chief Harper. They were done in half an hour. At least, that's when their truck left. Actually, one of them stayed behind, taking Chief Harper's air conditioner apart. It didn't look salvageable, but the guy was giving it his best shot.

He was doing it in street clothes. His work clothes left the police station in the van. Matt Greystone wore them. With a cap pulled down over his eyes, he looked quite natural in a repairman's gear. It occurred to Cora that might come in handy if his arm didn't heal.

The van dropped Matt off at home and no one was the wiser. Twenty minutes later he was seated at his dining room table with Jackie and Cora and Becky. Matt hadn't had time to shower, but he'd dunked his head in a sink full of water, and was consuming coffee at a rate that could not have been much faster had it been in an IV.

"Okay," Cora said. "Moment of truth time. You know that old joke where the guy says, 'You got any naked pictures of your wife?' The husband is shocked and says, 'Of course not!' The guy says, 'You want some?' "

"What the hell are you talking about?"

"Naked pictures of your wife. Leon Bratz had some."

"No, he didn't."

"Yeah, he did." Cora jerked his thumb at Jackie. "She claims she didn't know that."

Matt looked over at his wife. "Honey?"

Jackie put up her hands. "Don't look at me. This is all her idea."

"Yeah, but naked pictures?"

"She doesn't mean *now.* She's saying the guy found something in an old magazine. I don't think he did, but that's what she claims."

Matt blinked. "Wait a minute. You're saying there *are* naked pictures?"

"You want us to leave you two alone?" Becky said.

"No, I don't want you to leave us two alone," Matt said. "I want you to stop playing games and tell me what the hell is going on. I feel like my head's coming off. You

305

come in with a story like this, my wife isn't saying you're wrong. We've gotta get this straightened out before Don comes in and starts making fun of me."

"Don wouldn't do that," Jackie said.

Matt looked at her. "Are you telling me *he* knew?"

"Matt."

"Is the press going to know? Will that moron from the TV station ask me questions?"

"Not if we can help it," Becky said. "The police don't have this yet. Right now we're trying to prepare. Your wife says she doesn't know a thing, and I believe her. It's important, because the police will think it's a motive. And we'll be hard-pressed to prove she didn't know.

"Anyway, that's what the cops could have on your wife.

"Now for what the cops could have on you. Would you like to speak to me privately?"

"I have no secrets from my wife."

"I had no secrets from my ex-husband, Melvin," Cora said. "Of course, he hired a detective."

"Were you having an affair with Amanda Hoyt?" Becky said.

"Certainly not."

306

"Did you know her?"

"No, I didn't."

"Your name was on a file in her file cabinet."

"Honey?" Jackie said.

"I don't believe it. Show me the file."

"We don't have the file," Becky said.

"Of course, you don't. And you're not going to. This is nonsense, sweetheart. What would I want with a woman like that?" Matt grimaced. "Look. We're wasting time here. The main thing is protecting Jackie. If the police don't know about her, we've got to keep it that way. Can you do that?"

Cora sighed. "I can try."

CHAPTER 53

Stephanie grabbed the phone. "Yeah?"

"Is he awake?"

"I'm going to kill you."

"I don't want you to do anything, go anywhere, I'm not going to get you in trouble, is he awake?"

"I don't know how to answer that."

"A simple yes or no would suffice."

"When I get off the phone I'm either going to fall asleep, or he's going to roll over, sit up in bed, and say, 'Who was that?' As if he didn't know."

"I vote for the first choice."

"What am I going to tell him?"

"Tell him we've got to go to Yankee Stadium to interview a batboy who was checking invitations at Matt Greystone's party."

"What?"

"Yeah. I gotta do it anyway, I figured you and the sergeant would like to tag along. That's why I called."

"Why are you really calling?"

"I don't want you to get in any more trouble with Crowley."

"You and me both."

"So it would be better if he didn't know we broke into Leon Bratz's place."

"I hope he's not on the extension."

"Is there an extension?"

"No, but I'm getting spooky."

"So, there's absolutely no reason to bring it up."

"I'm with you there."

"So, you can't tell him about the naked pictures."

"Oh, so that's how it is."

"What, you were going to tell him about the naked pictures without telling him you broke in?"

In the background, a cranky, sleep-ridden voice growled, "Who the hell is that?"

"Cora's inviting us to Yankee Stadium."

CHAPTER 54

The guard at the Yankee Stadium press gate didn't want to let them in.

"You don't have tickets," he said.

"No," Sergeant Crowley said. "I have a shield." He flopped it open for the guard. "This is police business. We need to get in."

"Where would you watch the game from?"

"We're not going to watch the game. We just want to interview the batboy."

"I'll send him out. What's his name?"

"I don't know his name," Crowley said.

The guard looked at him suspiciously. "You don't know his name?"

"Of course we don't know his name," Cora said impatiently, "he's the batboy. It's not like he had stats and a uniform number and a rookie card. He picks up the goddamned bats."

Derek Jeter came out the door and spotted them. "Cora. What are you doing here?"

"Trying to get in. These are my friends,

Stephanie and Sergeant Crowley of the NYPD. This is Derek Jeter. Derek was at Matt's party. You know there's been another murder. We need to question the batboy who was checking invitations. The murdered woman was there that day, but she wasn't on the guest list."

"The woman with red hair?"

"Did she speak to you?"

"No, but she was hard to miss. They're taking batting practice now. He'll be out on the field. Come on, I'll take you out there. It's all right, Manny, they're with me."

Derek held the door open. Cora gave Manny her sweetest smile as she sailed through. Stephanie and Sergeant Crowley, visibly impressed, brought up the rear.

Derek led them through the locker room, empty now with everyone on the field, up the ramp, and into the dugout.

Players were milling around on the field, waiting their turn to bat. At the far end of the dugout, the batboy was filling the bat rack, making sure each player had his own personal bat.

"Hey, Danny," Derek said.

The batboy looked up.

"Come over here a minute."

"Oh, hi, Mr. Jeter. You wanna hit?"

"No, these people have some questions

for you."

Danny recognized Cora Felton. "You were at Matt's party."

"Yeah," Cora said. "And these guys are with the NYPD. They'd like to ask you a few questions."

"About what?"

"It's a little crowded in here," Cora said. "Could we step out on the field?"

"Not a good idea. You might get hit with a foul ball."

"Oh, God, I hope so," Cora said.

"You want a baseball?" Derek said. "Hey, Danny. Got some balls for our visitors?"

Danny hopped out of the dugout, retrieved some stray baseballs from the field.

Derek whipped out a pen, autographed them, and handed them to the guests. He took a little extra time with Cora's. She smiled, pushed it into her drawstring purse.

"Now then," Derek said, "if you stay just behind the screen here, I don't get in trouble and no one gets sued. I'm sure Danny would be glad to help you."

"Now, Danny," Cora said. "You were on the gate at Matt's party. You heard about the woman who got killed."

"I can't believe it," Danny said. "Such a nice lady."

"You remember her?"

"Oh, sure. With that red hair she's hard to miss."

"You checked her in at the gate?" Crowley said.

"Sure."

"But she wasn't on the guest list."

"That's right, she wasn't."

"Why'd you let her in?"

"She had an invitation."

"She had an invitation but she wasn't on the guest list?"

"That's right."

"How could that be?"

"I don't know."

"But you let her in?"

"Sure. That was my job. If someone was on the guest list, I let 'em in. If someone had an invitation, I let 'em in."

"Weren't the people who had invitations on the guest list?"

Danny nodded. "Most of 'em."

"Then why did you let her in?"

"Those were my instructions. If a person was on the guest list, let 'em in. If a person had an invitation, let 'em in. The woman wasn't on the guest list. I was going to ask Mrs. Greystone about her, but then she found her invitation."

"You didn't tell the police this when they questioned you at the Greystone house."

313

"She wasn't dead."

"All right, let me ask you this," Cora said. "Can you remember anyone else who wasn't on the guest list who had an invitation?"

Danny frowned. "Let me see. Hmm. As a matter of fact, there wasn't."

"Well, that was a waste of time," Crowley said as they left Yankee Stadium.

"Not at all," Cora said. "That was very interesting. The witch had an invitation but wasn't on the guest list. Now how do you think that happened?"

"She used someone else's invitation," Stephanie said promptly.

"Killjoy," Cora said. "Can't you come up with a sinister motive?"

Stephanie jerked her thumb at Crowley. "After years with him? Sinister motives are a dime a dozen. I can come up with several. But none more likely than she just used someone else's."

"She's got you there," Crowley said.

"Yeah. Except for one thing."

"What's that?"

"She's dead. She had an invitation, she wasn't on the list, and she's dead."

CHAPTER 55

Cora shook her head. "I can't make head nor tail of this case because nothing adds up. Matt has a car crash. I get a message to check Matt's brakes. I check Matt's brakes. There's nothing wrong with Matt's brakes.

"Then Matt's new car has an accident. Lo and behold, the brakes have been cut. Now the message makes sense. I've been told to check Matt's brakes and Matt's brakes have been cut. Except for one thing. When I got the message, Matt's brakes were fine. Someone sent me the message *before* Matt's brakes were cut. Was it the person who cut them? It seems to me that's the only one who would have known. So then why would they be warning me? So that Matt's brakes could be cut without killing Matt? Who does that benefit?

"Not to mention the fact that Matt isn't driving his car anyway. Most people know that. At least anyone involved with him. In particular his wife, who's the one who gave me the clue to begin with, and his agent, who winds up driving the car when it has the accident. Can you come up with a scenario for either one of them trying to kill Matt that makes sense?"

Becky put up her hand. "Trying to kill Matt, no. But that wasn't the premise. The premise was a reason to cut Matt's brakes. Murder does not have to be in mind."

"Fair enough," Cora said. "You come up with a reason for that."

"Oh, no," Becky said. "I'm not coming up with any reasons. I'm just picking holes in the ones you come up with."

"That's not particularly helpful," Cora said.

"Now you know how Chief Harper feels."

"Then we got the witch. According to the batboy, she had an invitation to the party. No one sent it, and yet it was there. As if that weren't spooky enough, she's got a file that said Matt Greystone. But it disappears. Right after someone stole her memory card. If she had a file for Matt in her file cabinet, you would think she had one on her computer. But that doesn't seem to be the case. And if she had appointments on the computer of her New York office, you would think there'd be appointments for Matt."

"Maybe he saw her under a different name."

"Best idea I've heard in a long time. And one we could actually check."

"If we had access to her computer files. Which we don't."

"Yeah, but the cops do."

"The cops are not inclined to be helpful right now."

"It depends on whether they're Yankees or Red Sox fans."

"Cora."

"Just sayin'."

"Anyway," Becky said. "If Matt was seeing the witch, how come he won't own up to it?"

"He's embarrassed about it?"

"I suppose so. It's the sort of thing the gossip columns could run with. It's an embarrassing bit of publicity. The type that agent of his tries to play down. And the type a sleazy journalist tries to play up. Hinting at voodoo rituals and the like. You know, blood sacrifices, biting the head off a live chicken. Who pays attention to such crap?"

"Clearly, you do."

"You can't help seeing the *National Enquirer* in the grocery line. Everybody does."

"The front page?"

"For the most part."

CHAPTER 56

"Hey, your air conditioner's working," Cora said.

"Yeah," Chief Harper said. "I like to think it's because I'm doing a fine job as chief and I really deserve it. But I realize it's only a side product of letting a prisoner escape."

"He didn't escape."

"Well, he's not here. And every reporter in town thought he was under arrest. What they think now is anybody's guess. Most of them are too responsible to make one, but Rick Reed's saying anything that comes to mind."

"Hold the phone. Breaking news. Chief Harper just expressed the opinion that Rick Reed actually has a mind. Film at eleven."

"It's not funny, Cora. This is a very sensitive case. The type of case where I can get in trouble just for doing my job."

"I understand."

"Do you? I'm glad to hear it, because I

don't understand. I feel I understand less the more this goes on."

"Maybe I can help you sort it out, Chief. I was thinking there might be a clue in the files in Amanda Hoyt's office."

"I thought you already saw those files."

"I didn't see those files. I saw that they existed, and then an overzealous night watchman nearly shot holes in me. If I had been able to look at those files, I might have been able to help you."

"Oh, would you now?"

"Absolutely. I was on the verge of a great discovery. Amanda Hoyt had a calendar on her computer, listing her appointments."

"And that's a great discovery?"

"It is, actually. The files of the witch's appointments go back a ways. I don't know how far back, because I don't know when she put in the program. But if her appointments included Matt Greystone, his name might be there. Because the calendar had nothing to do with the substance of her appointments, it's just a record of who showed up. So even if you couldn't get an account of what happened during the sessions, you could get a verification of the fact those sessions took place. Or at least *were scheduled* to take place, if you want to look at it like a prosecutor."

"That's an excellent idea. I will certainly pass it along."

"Chief."

"I can't let you into the woman's office to look at her computer files. Particularly when you've already been arrested for doing it."

"I think arrested is overstating it."

"Let's ask Sergeant Crowley. Did he or did he not put up bail?"

"Well, if you're going to fixate on every little thing."

"You know I can't let you into that office."

"I know."

"So why are you here?"

"It occurred to me you might be able to answer that question *without* letting me into that office."

"Oh, that occurred to you, did it?"

"Because the police would have been in that office and looked at that file. And if the name Matt Greystone jumped out, I would think that might be worthy of mention. So you'd know."

"You thought all that, did you?"

"Well, I can't take all the credit. Becky and I have been batting ideas around. Seeing as how she's the Greystones' attorney."

"She's representing both of them?"

"I see no reason why she should limit her

practice."

"Except for a conflict of interest."

"You mean you're charging only one? Or you mean you're charging both, but without the element of conspiracy? You figure if you can nail either one, you're batting five hundred."

"I'm not commenting on what the county prosecutor may or may not do. As you well know."

"Well, I'm commenting on what he might do, and I don't care if you quote me. He's charging Jackie Greystone. He's not charging Matt Greystone. Why? Well, not because he's got more evidence on her than on him. She doesn't pitch for the New York Yankees. He can convict her and send her to jail, and it won't affect the pennant race. Unless Matt becomes despondent and can't pitch."

"He has a broken arm."

"Broken arms mend. Broken hearts don't."

"Oh, please."

"Too corny? Damn. I was thinking it might be a country western song. Of course I'm not sure too corny's a deal breaker."

Harper frowned, cocked his head. "Cora, I know you. When you get this manic, it's because you're fresh out of ideas."

Cora sighed. "Damned if I'm not. You

don't think telling me about Matt Greystone's appointments might give me a jump
start?"

"Sorry, Cora."

"All right, if you can't tell me about the
file, can you tell me about the gun?"

"What gun?"

"Come on. You got a woman dead by
gunshot wound. What gun do you think I
mean?"

"No, I can't tell you about the gun."

"You haven't done the ballistics test?"

"I don't do the ballistics test. We send it
out to the lab."

"That's all right. You don't have to tell me
about the gun. Either you don't have the
results yet, which I would find hard to
believe, or neither of the guns was the
murder weapon. Because if it was Don's
gun, you'd be celebrating like it was the
Fourth of July all over again, and the Greystones would be free to go. And if it was
Matt's gun, I wouldn't even be able to get
in here because you'd all be running around
like chickens with their heads cut off. And
Ratface would be having delusions of gran-
deur and practicing up for his TV appear-
ances. And I can't believe you didn't get the
tests expedited, so I'm going with neither
gun. Any comment on that?"

Dan Finley burst in the door. "We found the gun!"

CHAPTER 57

"Are you representing Don?" Cora said.

Becky shrugged. "I can't represent Don unless they dismiss the charges against Jackie."

"Any chance of that happening?"

"Do you think the prosecutor's going to do that just to accommodate me?"

"Well, if he wants to date you."

"Cora, that's not funny. He's got a case against Don and he's also got a case against Jackie. Ordinarily, that would be tough for him, but there happens to be two crimes."

"You had no problem representing Matt and Jackie."

"They happen to be man and wife. And there was no theory they acted alone. They could be considered coconspirators."

"But she was the only one charged."

"Because he's a star pitcher, and Henry Firth didn't want to stick his neck out. But that's his problem. I think about representing them and I have no problem. On the other hand, I think about representing Jackie and Don and, oh, my God. Are the two of them an item and her husband's out? Are the two of them acting as coconspirators? Not in a million years. And if Jackie didn't kill Leon Bratz, there's a chance Don did. A damn good chance. I know it. Henry Firth knows it. And wouldn't that be wonderful, because neither of them pitch."

"Don pitches."

"In the minor leagues. No one *cares* about the minor leagues."

"What's Don say about the gun?"

"I can't ask Don about the gun because I'm not his attorney. I can ask my clients about the gun, but they don't know anything. If I asked Don, he'd probably say he didn't know anything, either."

Jackie Greystone burst into the office. "You've got to represent Don!"

"I can't."

"You've got to. He didn't do it."

"How do you know?"

"I just know."

"That's not good enough."

"I just talked to him."

"I told you not to do that."

"Yeah, I know. But this is serious."

Becky rolled her eyes. "Oh, my God, I'm

a hundred years old. I'm playing nursemaid to a bunch of naughty kids."

"You can't leave Don with no attorney at all."

"He'll call someone in New York."

"And meanwhile he just sits there?"

The search of Don's rental car had discovered a gun stashed under the driver's seat. Ballistics tests had determined it was indeed the gun that killed Amanda Hoyt. Cogent legal analysis by crack investigative reporter Rick Reed was that Don was toast.

"This is silly," Jackie said. "If they think it was Don, they can't think it was me."

"Not a chance."

"Why not?"

"As long as I'm representing you, I can't represent him. The prosecutor knows that. He would much rather keep me off the case."

"You're that good?"

"She is, but that's not why," Cora said. "If the case comes to trial, the prosecutor will be presenting it to a jury of Bakerhaven residents. They happen to like Becky Baldwin, and they won't want to see him destroy her in court. On the other hand, they'd be all too happy to see him rip some smug New York attorney's can off."

Jackie looked at Becky. "Is she serious?"

"Cora tends to overstate the case, but the principle is valid. Don's an outsider. If his attorney's an outsider, he's got two strikes against him."

"You're just proving why he needs you."

Becky looked at Cora. "You didn't think that one through, did you?"

"Well, it sounded good," Cora said.

"Can't you shame him into letting me go?" Jackie said.

"How?"

"Just what she said. Go on TV and say that's why he won't."

"I can't do that," Becky said.

Cora clapped her hands together. "No. But you can say you're *not* doing that."

Chapter 58

"This is Rick Reed, Channel 8 News, live in Bakerhaven, the scene of two shocking crimes. Earlier today we broke the news that the gun used in the killing of Amanda Hoyt had been discovered concealed under the driver's seat of the rental car of Don Upton, a minor league pitcher and former teammate of Yankee superstar Matt Greystone. Ballistics tests have shown it to be the murder weapon used in the killing of Bakerhaven resident Amanda Hoyt, and Don Upton has been placed in police custody.

"Speculation has run rife that crack courtroom specialist Becky Baldwin would be stepping up to represent Don Upton in his defense of this capital crime. But to this reporter's surprise, such is not the case.

"Miss Baldwin. Do I understand correctly that you are not Don Upton's lawyer?"

"No, I am not."

"You refused to represent him? Is that

because you think he is guilty?"

"No, and no. I haven't *refused* to represent him. I'm not *eligible* to represent him because I'm representing Jackie Greystone."

"But Jackie Greystone didn't do anything."

"I'm certainly glad to hear it. If you could pass the word on to county prosecutor Henry Firth, I'd be extremely grateful."

"Does he think they were acting in concert?"

"I can't comment on what the prosecutor may or may not think. But I can't believe anyone could possibly think they were acting in concert."

"Then why hasn't he released her?"

"Again, I can't comment on what the prosecutor has in mind. One explanation I've heard advanced is that he doesn't want to meet me in court. That he won't release Jackie Greystone until Don Upton is forced to find another attorney. Personally, I can't believe that for a moment. I know Henry Firth. Such crass manipulations are beneath him. I'm sure he will speak up soon and put an end to such vile accusations. For my part, my only concern is that no one should misinterpret the fact that I am not representing Don Upton and think it reflects badly on the young man. I would be perfectly happy to represent him were I free to do so."

"Despite the fact Don Upton and Matt Greystone were discharging firearms at the scene of the crime on the very day it occurred?"

Becky smiled. "In court a question like that would draw a barrage of objections. Leading and suggestive, assuming facts not in evidence. Since we're not in court I can only ask, were you referring to guns that had nothing to do with the murder? Because if you were, I have it on good authority they were also considering ordering a pizza that had nothing to do with the murder either."

Rick Reed blinked.

"But we're getting off topic, Rick. The main point is I don't for a minute believe that county prosecutor Henry Firth is afraid to meet me in court."

CHAPTER 59

Becky Baldwin sized up the cocky young man sitting across from her. "The prosecutor has dismissed the charges against Jackie Greystone."

"So I understand."

"I am therefore free to defend you. Please understand, I am not soliciting employment. I am merely saying that due to the change in the situation, I am now available."

"I can't afford you."

"Matt Greystone has offered to put up your retainer."

"Isn't that a conflict of interest? In case you want to pin the murder on him?"

"I don't want to pin the murder on him. I don't want to pin the murder on anyone. I'm not that type of attorney. If someone's guilty, I have no problem saying they did it. But I'm not about to attack an innocent man just to raise reasonable doubt."

"So you can only represent me with qualifications?"

"You'd like an attorney who *would* implicate an innocent party?"

"I'd like an attorney whose concern is to represent me, not someone who'd be hesitant to raise the concept someone else might have done it."

"That's not what I'm saying and you know it. I may not look like it, but I've been doing this for a while. I know who I can and can't represent. I also operate under my own set of ethics, and I don't do something just because I can get away with it. And I don't *fail* to do something just because it's not in *my* best interests. I do what's best for my client, and I'll throw Matt Greystone's fee back in his face if he tries to get me to do something that in my opinion is not in *your* best interests. If you want me, fine. If you don't want me, fine. If you want to talk this out and see if you want me, that's fine, too. Everything you tell me is confidential, even if you decide you're not going to hire me. You're approaching me as a client, and everything you tell me is privileged. You want to give it a whirl?"

"Well, when you put it like that."

"How'd the gun get in your car?"

"I assume someone put it there. That's assuming it *was* in my car. Just because

332

someone says it was doesn't make it so."

"Was your car locked?"

"No."

"The police say it was."

"And the police say the gun was in it. That would make both of those statements suspect."

"How do you know it wasn't locked?"

"I didn't lock it. It's a rental car. On a friend's property. There was nothing in it. Why would I lock it?"

"You'd lock it if you stashed a gun there."

"Yeah, right. If I had a murder weapon that wasn't mine and couldn't be connected to me in any way, I'd lock it up in my own rental car so in case it was found it *would* connect to me. That would not make me the swiftest murderer that ever lived."

"Killers often panic."

"I don't."

"Ever kill someone?"

"Is that a clever trap?"

"Jackie Greystone used to be your girlfriend."

Don blinked. "Nice change of subject."

"She was your girlfriend and she married Matt. Did that cause any tension between the two of you?"

"You know it did."

"How would I know that?"

"Because you know enough to ask the question. And you were her attorney. Or are you still?"

"I'm flexible."

"Oh, really?"

Becky made a face. "Oh, please. Don't try to be irrepressible. I get enough of that from my investigator."

CHAPTER 60

Aaron Grant shoved a forkful of lamb couscous into his mouth. "Oh, hell."

"Daddy said 'hell,' " Jennifer said.

"No, Jennifer did," Cora said.

"Tattletale," Jennifer said.

"Hush," Sherry said.

"Mommy said 'hush.' "

" 'Hush' isn't a bad word," Sherry said.

"No," Cora said. "You want to hear some bad words, Jennifer?"

"Cora."

"Just trying to clear up any confusion."

"She's a child."

"I'm a big girl!"

"See, she's a big girl," Cora said.

"Daddy's going to say something a lot worse if someone doesn't answer me," Aaron said. "I've been losing to Rick Reed all week. Becky keeps changing clients every half hour. The police keep changing who they're charging. And we've got more murder weapons arriving every minute. The whole Yankee telecast this evening will be on anything but baseball, and whoever wins the game will be entirely coincidental. Now, I appreciate eating dinner in front of a TV we can mute when the commercials come on, but right now I'd be happy muting Rick Reed. Is there anything I can write that he doesn't have?"

Cora shook her head. "Dan Finley slips him stuff before I even get it."

"Well, can you tell me who Becky's representing."

"I'm not sure *Becky* can tell you who she's representing. I think the way it works is she's representing Matt Greystone, Jackie Greystone, or Don Upton, depending on who's charged with the crime."

"And just who is accused of the crime at the moment?"

"At the moment it's Don Upton," Cora said. "But that's subject to change in the event someone goes on the DL and he gets called up to the majors."

"And a gun was planted in his car?"

"Whoa, listen to the biased reporting. I'd watch out, Sherry. He's ready to believe anyone's innocent if Becky represents them."

"Big deal, so am I," Sherry said. "I think

everyone's going to be very unhappy with this case."

"Why?" Cora said.

"Everything points to the fact Matt did it. No one wants that. But he's got the money, the power, and the fame. Those are the type of people who have something to hide, and those are the type of people who kill."

"Matt did it!" Jennifer squealed.

"Oh, my God," Cora said. "Now look what you've done. Just let Rick Reed get a hold of *that* sound bite."

"Bite!" Jennifer squealed.

"That's not a bad word," Cora said. "You have to say 'bite *me.*' "

"Bite me!"

"Cora, I'm going to kill you."

"Mommie's going to kill Aunt Cora!"

"And you complain about me," Cora said. "You're training her to be a witness for the prosecution."

"Seriously," Aaron said, "how are we going to get out of it?"

"We? I'm not in it."

"How is this ever going to end?"

"I don't think it is. Becky is just going to keep racking up retainers until she's ready to retire. I'm not sure what happens to the defendants then, but someone is sure to step up."

"You're bluffing," Aaron said.

Cora looked at him. "I beg your pardon."

"You're sitting here looking like you're not concerned, and Matt Greystone is involved in a murder case. He may not be the current suspect, but it doesn't matter, the case revolves around him. I know it, you know it, everybody else knows it. And you're going nuts trying to figure the whole thing out so he can pitch again as soon as possible. Knowing you, you'll come up with some convoluted way to do it, which won't appear to make any sense to any normal rational person, but which will turn out to be diabolically clever, revealing the killer and making everyone slap their foreheads saying, 'My God, why didn't I think of it'?"

"Is that what you think I'm doing?" Cora said.

"I know that's what you're doing."

"The hell I am."

"Cora said 'hell'!"

"No, Jennifer did."

Sherry exhaled in exasperation.

"Mommy almost said it, too."

"What?" Cora said.

Sherry pointed at the TV.

It was a commercial for one of the fantasy baseball sites that were all the rage. Fans picked their teams of players, and got paid off depending on how they performed. It was just like the fantasy baseball people always played, except you had to pay to do it.

"I can't believe Major League Baseball is sponsoring these rip-off artists," Sherry said. "It's gambling, plain and simple. It's betting on baseball. They ban Pete Rose for betting on baseball, and here they are promoting gambling. It's shameful."

Cora frowned. "Pete Rose," she murmured.

"What about Pete Rose?" Aaron said.

"Could it really be that simple?"

"Simple?" Aaron said. "Did you just figure out who did it?"

"No," Cora said. "But it wouldn't be a bad idea to pretend I did."

"Cora," Sherry said.

But Cora was already rushing out the door.

Chapter 61

"I want to get into the witch's house."

Chief Harper cocked his head at Cora. "Oh? Well, guess what?"

Cora waved it away. "Yeah, yeah, I know. You're about to get a big kick out of denying me access to the witch's house. But here's the deal. We're not making any progress, every time you turn around you've got a new suspect, and the town's in danger of becoming a laughingstock. You've got to do something to crack this case open."

"Of course, I do. And since I won't let you into Amanda Hoyt's office, now you want to get into her house."

"That's not it at all."

"Oh? Tell me, where did I go wrong?"

"What a setup. I got too many answers to that, Chief. But I happen to be your friend. I'm not trying to pull a fast one. I'm trying to clear away some of the deadwood. I don't just want you to let me into the witch's house. I want you there. And Matt Grey-stone. And his wife. And his agent. And his friend. And a few other people. I want them all on hand."

"What for?"

Cora grimaced. "See, this is where it's bet-ter if you take me on faith. I'm hoping to trap a killer, but if I don't, I'd rather have you poking fun at me after the event instead of before."

"Cora, this is not coming out well."

"Yeah, I know. Chief, you ever have a case you didn't wanna solve?"

"What do you mean?"

"You know what I mean. You got a murder case. You figure it out. Then you wish you hadn't."

"What are you trying to tell me?"

"No matter who you charge, the case looks bad for Matt Greystone. The longer it's open the more he gets hurt. You got to solve it and get him off the hook."

"Oh, now I'm a stumbling block in the way of the Yankees winning the pennant?"

"Well, not this year. He's not coming back this year. The question is whether he comes back at all. You can make that happen, but you got to have a little faith."

"And what do you expect Henry Firth to think of your little scheme?"

"Ask him."

"What?"

"Ask him. Invite him to be there. It's a win-win for Ratface. He gets all the suspects assembled, he gets to hear what they say, and no one's invoking any nasty rights to remain silent. Becky Baldwin will be there to give it her blessing, so there will be no question of anyone violating anyone's rights."

Cora lowered her voice. "Plus, you don't have to tell anyone we're doing it. I certainly won't. And you won't. And Henry won't. And if you can stop Dan Finley from tipping Rick Reed, we can do the whole thing under the radar. And if it doesn't work, no harm, no foul. Sorry, wrong sports metaphor. But you know what I mean.

"We gotta do something. No one's happy with the current situation. Except maybe a few Red Sox fans. But even they feel bad for the kid. One tragedy on top of another. It's enough to drive anybody around the bend, let alone a young man in his situation. Just give me a shot."

Chief Harper studied Cora's face. "I can't remember you ever so impassioned about anything."

"Hey, I'm a Yankee fan. I admit it. But that's not what this is all about. Well, maybe a little. I'm afraid my judgment's impaired because of who he is. I have to do something to compensate. This is my shot. I've gotta take it. If I can't persuade you to cooperate I'll probably have a nervous breakdown, and I have to tell you the resultant fallout is not going to be beneficial to the police department."

Cora smiled her most ingratiating smile. "So, please, help me out here. Get me into the witch's house."

Harper considered. "All right. What do you have in mind?"

Cora grimaced. "I'd rather not say."

CHAPTER 62

"This is my first séance," Cora said. "So please forgive me if I'm not entirely professional. I've never raised the dead before, so I can't promise that they'll cooperate."

Cora looked around at the faces of the people assembled in the witch's drawing room. They ranged, in Cora's estimation, from the skeptical to the more skeptical.

Seated around the table were: Matt Greystone; Jackie Greystone; Don Upton; Matt's agent, Lenny; Matt's real estate agent, Judy Douglas Knauer; Becky Baldwin; Chief Harper; and Cora Felton.

Henry Firth stood a step back from the table, arms folded, as if divorcing himself from the proceedings. Having been talked into going, the prosecutor was not at all happy when he got there and discovered the nature of the event to which he had allowed Chief Harper to escort the prisoner. Cora counted herself lucky he hadn't immediately pulled the plug.

"Anyway," Cora said, "since I've never contacted the dead before, I don't expect to be able to do anything spectacular, like voices, or holograms, or levitations, or anything of that ilk. Of course, if a spirit wants to chime in, they will certainly be welcome. But all I'm shooting for is a push in the right direction. A hint as to what the hell happened. Because clearly nobody knows. And I don't think the police are getting any closer to the truth, no matter how many people they arrest. And I'd hate for us to become a laughingstock. Which is a very real possibility. We have a multimillion-dollar pitcher here, which guarantees attention will be focused on Bakerhaven until something is resolved.

"As if that weren't enough reason to resort to the supernatural, consider this. Puzzles have been interjected into these crimes. I take that personally. It's like someone threw down the gauntlet. Under such circumstances I really hate to admit that I haven't a clue.

"Well, I'm admitting it, I'm desperate, and I'm ready to try anything.

"Anyway, I'm going to do the best I can. And I need you all to help me. This doesn't work if there are nonbelievers." Cora put up

her hand. "I know, I know, you're all nonbelievers. So am I. But I'm going to give it my
best shot, and I ask you to give it yours.

"Since I can't do the spectacular, I'm going to try to do something simple. I found
this wooden box."

Cora picked the box up, set it on the table.

"It was hidden in the attic in a trunk
labeled 'Do Not Touch.' Naturally, I did.
Which probably means I'm cursed. Anyway,
I found this Ouija board."

Cora pulled a wooden Ouija board out of
the box.

"The witch had stashed it in this wooden
chest with the admonition not to open it,
and probably never thought of it again.
Which makes it perfect for our purpose. It
is a neutral Ouija board, untainted by the
witch's use. It will not slant things in her
favor."

"Oh, my God!" Don said. "I'm sitting
here listening, trying to go along, but this is
too much. Untainted by the witch's use?
What kind of hooey are you peddling here?"

"Now, Don," Jackie said. "This is an old-
fashioned séance, plain and simple. Buy the
premise, buy the bit. No one's asking you
to believe in this nonsense. We're asking you
to shut up and let it happen."

"And a more ringing endorsement was

346

never uttered," Cora said. "If we could all heed the words of Jackie Greystone and co-operate, I'd like to get out of here. There's a Yankee game tonight.

"All right, let's give it a try. Let's all put our hands on the thingy. That's probably not the official name, but you know what I mean. The wooden pointer that slides across the Ouija board and spells out the words. That's it, crowd around, touch it with one hand. You don't have to grip it hard, you just have to make contact.

"Are you ready? Here we go."

Cora looked up, frowned. "Spirits. I'm new at this and I need your help. To begin with, is anybody here?"

There was a pause.

Everyone stared at the pointer.

After a few minutes it began to move.

"Look!" Judy Douglas Knauer said.

The pointer slid around the board.

"Who's pushing it?" Don said. "You're not supposed to push it."

"No one's pushing it," Cora said.

"How can you tell?"

"Because that would defeat the whole purpose, and no one wants to do that."

The pointer slid across the board and stopped at Yes.

"Who is trying to contact me?"

The pointer slid again.

It stopped on L.

Then E.

Then O.

Then N.

"Ah," Cora said. "The spirit of someone who has recently passed over. I wonder if that's easier, or just more appropriate. Let's cut to the chase. Leon. Who killed you?"

There was a long pause.

Then the pointer began to move.

D.

O.

N.

Don was up out of his chair. "All right, that's it. I'm out of here. I didn't kill anybody. And I'm not going to let some children's toy tell me I did."

"Look!" Jackie cried.

The pointer was moving again. It had really never stopped. After spelling Don it continued writing. It glided across the board, stopped on:

T.

"It's not him," Jackie said. "His last name doesn't start with 'T.' "

"Whose name does?" Chief Harper said.

The pointer was still moving. It stopped on:

K.

" 'K'? TK?" Harper said. "No one's name starts TK."

"Unless 'T' is the middle initial," Judy suggested.

The pointer continued moving.

N.

O.

W.

" 'Now'?" Matt said. "Why 'now'?"

"Not 'now,' " Cora said. " 'Know.' The answer is, 'DON'T KNOW.' Leon doesn't know who killed him. Disappointing, but there you are."

"Well, why the hell would he bother to contact us just to tell us that?" Matt said.

"Maybe he can help us in another way," Jackie said.

Matt looked at her. "You're buying this?"

"Did the pointer move or not?"

"It's a trick."

"Leon," Cora said. "Can you help us in another way?"

The pointer moved.

No.

"Well, this was a waste of time," Lenny said.

"We're not done yet," Cora said.

"Yeah, well, hurry up, will you? As if two murders weren't enough to deal with. If it gets out that Matt's using a Ouija board . . ."

Lenny shook his head.

"He's not using a Ouija board," Harper said. "Cora Felton is trying an experiment in the hope of helping the police."

"Oh, yeah," Lenny said. "You watch it on the evening news you'd think Matt Greystone *invented* the Ouija board."

"Is anybody trying to contact me?" Cora said.

The pointer moved again.

Yes.

"Who's there?" Cora said.

A.

M.

A.

N.

" 'A man,' " Don said. "That's a little nonspecific."

D.

A.

" 'Amanda,' " Cora said. "That's the name of the other victim. Surely you know that."

"I did. I'm joking. This whole thing is a big joke."

"Do you have something to tell us?" Cora asked.

The pointer moved.

Yes.

"Do you know who killed you?"

Yes.

"Are you going to tell us?"

Yes.

"Who was it?"

The pointer moved.

L.

E.

Lenny sprang from his seat. "Oh, no you don't! You're not going to pin this on me!"

The pointer was moving inexorably toward the N.

It passed by and stopped on:

O.

It went back and stopped on:

N.

" 'Leon,' " Cora said. "She's accusing Leon Bratz."

"Impossible," Harper said. "Leon Bratz died first."

"How do you know?" Cora said.

Time stopped still. People looked at each other. Mental calculations were made. Memories were traced. Had Amanda Hoyt been seen after the discovery of the body of Leon Bratz?

Cora clapped her hands together. "Lights."

Nothing happened.

"Oh, right," Cora said. "We're all at the table. There's no one to turn on the lights.

I'll have to find 'em myself."

Cora snapped her fingers.

The lights went on.

Cora smiled. "Hey, I'm getting good at this. I may have another profession if the puzzle thing fails. All right, that's the show for tonight. Your homework for tomorrow: figure out the last time you saw Amanda Hoyt alive. Was it at the party? Was it after the party? If it was at the party, was it before or after the body of Leon Bratz was discovered? Is there any chance, however slim, that during the party Leon Bratz lured Amanda Hoyt into the woods, shot her, and stashed the gun in Don's car, and returned to the party just in time to get murdered in the sauna bath? That's your homework. As for tonight, I would say it all went relatively well."

Cora shrugged. "But I'm not quitting my day job."

Chapter 63

Chief Harper could hardly contain himself. "What the hell did you think you were doing?"

"Holding a séance."

"I know you were holding a séance. What are you doing accusing the victim of the crime?"

"One of the victims. Of one of the crimes. It's a no-no in mystery books, but that doesn't mean it doesn't happen."

Cora and Chief Harper were back at the police station rehashing the séance. Henry Firth had declared it a colossal waste of time, and gone off to bed.

"You seriously think Leon Bratz killed Amanda Hoyt?"

"Well, now you're quibbling."

"Quibbling! You just presented an impossibility. You stated it as fact. You asked the witnesses to go home and think about it."

"*Is* it an impossibility, Chief? Have *you*

thought back to the last time *you* saw Amanda Hoyt alive?"

"I don't have to think back. You're talking about a physical impossibility. Barney Nathan could tell you that in his sleep."

Harper blushed, perhaps remembering that Cora had had occasion to observe Barney Nathan in his sleep.

"A child of ten could tell you that, Chief. Amanda Hoyt died at least a day later. What's your point?"

"The point is it didn't happen. And your grand and glorious séance is a resounding sham."

Cora's eyes twinkled. "You thought it was going to be real, Chief?"

"Did you really find that Ouija board in the witch's attic?"

"I bought it at Kelly's Antiques."

"What did you accomplish?"

"Some rather keen insights into the personalities and temperaments of the main participants."

"You mean Don?"

"Don is certainly one of them."

"Who else did you mean?"

"Come on, Chief, I don't want to do all your work for you. The point is, you got a whole bunch of people there, and you got to sort out the motives. Who had the most to gain? Who had the most to lose?"

"All right, who did?"

"You're not going to like the answer."

"Why not?"

"You just won't."

"All right, what's the answer?"

"Judy Douglas Knauer."

Chief Harper dropped his coffee. It reminded Cora of Chazz Palminteri in *The Usual Suspects* dropping his coffee cup in slow motion.

"Judy Douglas Knauer?"

"Yeah."

"Had the best motive?"

"In terms of financial gain. I'm not saying she did it."

"How in the world do you figure that?"

"A little research, actually. Matt Greystone's buying his house."

"He bought it."

"That's what everybody thought. But the deal is not finalized. At the moment he is renting it with an *option* to buy. Huge difference, if you are a real estate broker and work on commissions. The commission on that house would put Judy Douglas Knauer on easy street. If the deal goes through, she's a very happy lady. If the deal goes south, she takes a colossal hit. Leon Bratz was a huge fly in the ointment. Matt had come up here for a quiet rehab. If Leon was going to hound him here, maybe Matt would decide it was too close to the City and pull up stakes."

"Are you serious?"

"About the motive, yes. I don't for a moment think Judy Douglas Knauer did it."

"But you had her at the séance."

"Well, I had to have someone. I couldn't make it look like we were ganging up on the four outsiders."

"But that's who it is, isn't it? Matt, Jackie, Lenny, and Don. It's one of them. You know it. I know it. Isn't that who it is?"

"Unless it's a player to be named later."

Harper looked at her. "Are you trying to be funny?"

"Well, why not? Matt's the player to be named later. Why not the killer to be named later?"

"Do you mean it?"

"No."

"So what did you learn from your séance?"

"Nothing I can repeat."

"What do you mean by that?"

"Well, I wouldn't want to get sued for slander."

"You can't get sued for slander for telling me."

"Tell that to Becky Baldwin."

"Come on, Cora. It's just the two of us here. If you know who did it, you want to let me in?"

"I don't know who did it. I have nothing more than a hunch."

"That's all you ever have."

"Gee, thanks a lot."

"I didn't mean it that way."

"I think you did, Chief. I think you're frustrated and lashing out."

"Oh, for goodness sakes." Chief Harper caught the twinkle in her eye. "You're having fun with me."

"Well, I have to have fun with something. A Yankee superstar moves into town, and all I've got is grief. People pester me with puzzles."

"And what's that all about?" Harper said. "Why would the killer leave a puzzle at the crime relating to a totally different incident? Unless it's Matt Greystone and he's telling you to check his brakes in an incredible double bluff to make you think he's not the killer."

"My God, Chief, you've been hanging out with me for too long. Did you really just say that?"

"I did, but only for lack of anything better. You wanna tell me how that puzzle winds up in that sauna?"

"Probably not."

"What do you mean?"

"Well, the way this case is developing, I don't think I can. I think it's entirely possible we can uncover the killer and never find out what the puzzle meant. And that's okay. There's no legal precedent saying you can't get a conviction unless you solve a puzzle. If there was, there'd be a lot fewer men on death row."

"You're joking again?"

"Barely. I'm frustrated, too, Chief. I'm happy to have Matt Greystone in town, but I'd far prefer him at the ballpark pitching the Yankees into the World Series. Anyway, we had a séance, and it was interesting, but inconclusive. So I think we have to try again."

"Another séance?"

"Hell, no. I'd rather be shot dead."

"So what did you have in mind?"

"A town meeting."

"And how will that help you?"

"It will help me unmask the killer."

"How will that unmask the killer?"

"It won't. But the killer will think it would."

"So?"

"While his attention's distracted, we can

pull a fast one."

"*We* can pull a fast one?"

"Well, sure, Chief. I wasn't going to leave you out."

"Leave me out of what, Cora? What do you have in mind?"

"While everyone's attention is diverted, you'll step up and arrest the killer."

"You know who the killer is?"

"I always know who the killer is." Cora smiled. "I'm just not always right."

CHAPTER 64

The town hall was packed. There was no room for TV cameras, though Rick Reed managed to sneak in a mobile feed from a mini unit. His camera crew wasn't let in, but he bribed a kid from town.

Everyone else was there. Every seat was taken, and standing room was at a premium. The only ones who weren't crowded were Matt and Jackie Greystone, Don Upton, and Lenny Schick. They sat in the front row, flanked by officers Dan Finley and Sam Brogan. The policemen appeared to be escorting the prisoner, but they were also strategically located to keep any of the suspects from leaving.

Cora stood at the front of the crowd. "All right, ladies and gentlemen. You all know why I called this meeting. Two crimes have disrupted our way of life. We'd like to clear them up and go back to the way we were. Of course, there's no real going back to the way we were, because now we have a celebrity. We can go back to the way we were when we had a celebrity and no one was dead. The only real way we could go back to the way we were would be if we were to convict Matt Greystone of the crime. Then we could return to the sleepy little town we all love."

Lenny Schick was on his feet. "That's outrageous. Matt doesn't have to sit and listen to that kind of talk."

"Of course not," Cora said. "He can get up and storm out. But he's not that type of guy. He is, from everything I've observed, a real nice guy. A decent fellow. A good neighbor. A person you'd be very happy to have living next door to you. I cannot imagine anyone arranging murders on his estate to drive him out of town."

Lenny blinked. "What are you talking about?"

"Oh, virtually nothing, as usual. I just want to explain to everyone what's going on here. Because people don't know. You do, because you were there last night, but as far as everyone else is concerned.

"We had a séance last night to try to figure out who the killer was. We had it at Amanda Hoyt's house, because she was one of the victims, and because she had a reputation

361

for the occult. We tried to contact Amanda and find out who killed her. I must say she was less than helpful. Not that she didn't name her killer. She did. She named Leon Bratz as her killer. That was particularly unhelpful, seeing as how Leon Bratz died first. And dead men don't go around killing people, even if the crime is occult."

Harvey Beerbaum rose to his feet. The pudgy cruciverbalist looked miffed, perhaps at being left out of the séance. "Hang on there, Cora. You are saying Amanda Hoyt *named* her killer?"

"That's right. She did it with a Ouija board rather than a voice, but she named him nonetheless. Ever since we've been trying to figure out who saw Amanda Hoyt alive after Leon Bratz was dead. So far no one's certain. I'm sure it's just because no one had a reason to think of it before, so I am happy for this opportunity to ask all of you. If there is anyone who remembers definitely seeing Amanda Hoyt alive after Leon Bratz was found dead, please come forward."

No one did.

"Of course not. No one remembers because it wasn't important. It wasn't important then, and it isn't important now. It's an idiotic notion. Leon Bratz died long before

Amanda Hoyt, despite what some children's toy might say. The medical evidence will prove it conclusively. But I don't need the medical evidence. And I don't need a witness to the fact that Leon Bratz didn't kill Amanda Hoyt. I happen to know Leon Bratz didn't kill Amanda Hoyt because I happen to know who did."

Cora glanced around the room. "No one's particularly impressed. You figure I'm bluffing. That this is some clever scheme on my part to get the murderer to reveal himself. I don't play that way. Well, actually I do, but not this time. This time the murderer is obvious. In a mystery novel, it would be considered disappointing. Luckily, we don't care. We just want the crime solved, so we can go about our business.

"Dan Finley, stand up."

The young officer rose to his feet to a murmur of voices.

Cora put up her hand. "Relax. It's not Dan. I'm merely setting the stage. Sam Brogan, stand up. And, no, it's not him, either. I don't want them to have to spring up to make the arrest.

"First of all, I'm happy to announce there is only one killer. That is to say, the killer of Amanda Hoyt and Leon Bratz is one and the same person."

Cora glanced around. "All right, Don. Would you stand up?"

Don rose to his feet with a sardonic grin. "I hope you're positioning me to catch the killer. If you're accusing me of the crime, I can't say I think very highly of your abilities."

"No one's accusing anyone of anything," Cora said. "Yet," she added. "Don is Matt's old friend. Used to room together on the road when they were on the same team in the minor leagues.

"Lenny, stand up. A lot of you may not have met Lenny, but you saw him on the Fourth of July when he showed up in the limo Matt was supposed to take."

Cora clapped her hands together. "All right, if you would please remain standing, I am now going to solve the crime. I welcome you all to solve it along with me. Here's a hint. Just because someone is standing, doesn't mean they did it. It doesn't mean they didn't, and it doesn't mean they did. The killer might well be sitting. In other words, we are not limiting the suspects to people on their feet. So, come on, take a stab at it.

"If you're wrong, don't feel bad. It isn't easy. I must say this crime gave me a lot of trouble.

"One thing that *really* gave me trouble was the crossword puzzle left at the crime scene. Killers often do this to taunt me. I don't know why. It's a stupid idea. Inevitably it helps me catch them. And yet they will not be dissuaded. They think they're too smart for me. They may well be, but there's other ways to show it.

"One way would be, *not* leaving a crossword puzzle. That's what the killer did in this case, and that's what gave me trouble. Because I'd fallen into the same old rut. I'd assumed if there's a crossword, it was left by the killer. The crossword puzzle left in the sauna was actually left by the *victim.*

"So, had Leon Bratz just left the crossword puzzle when he was surprised and killed? Not at all. Leon Bratz was surprised and killed, and with his dying breath, Leon Bratz reached into his jacket pocket, grabbed the crossword puzzle, and thrust it up, hoping it would point to his killer.

"Unfortunately, it fell from his hand into the stove, making it look as if it had been left instead *by* the killer.

"Are you following all that? It's all right, it doesn't matter. Because I am now going to do what Leon Bratz was unable to do. I am going to point to the killer. And that killer is . . ."

The lights went out.

CHAPTER 65

There were cries, whispering, nervous laughter, all the sorts of things you could associate with a blackout. It went on for fifteen or twenty seconds, though it seemed much longer in the darkness.

And then, as abruptly as they had gone out, all the lights came on again.

Cora looked around the room. Raised her hands for silence. It took awhile for people to quiet down. When they had, she shrugged. "Well, it didn't work. The killer was supposed to get up in the dark and try to escape. That didn't happen. Which is really bad. It makes me oh for two. *It looked extremely rocky for the Mudville nine that day.*

"So what you gonna do? You gonna stay with 'Casey at the Bat'? I don't think so. We all know how that worked out. If I'm mighty Casey, I'm gonna swing and miss. So I'm gonna bring in a pinch hitter. Chief Harper. A man who has quietly piled up the best batting average in the league. And his on-base average is fantastic, when you consider the times he's been intentionally walked. Going with the metaphor, that's the defendant copping a plea. Anyway —" Cora leaned close to the microphone, and simulated a loud speaker echo. "Now batting for Cora Felton, number forty-four, Chief Dale Harper, Harper, Harper, Harper."

Chief Harper stepped up to the microphone. Unlike the Puzzle Lady, he didn't indulge himself in any dramatics, just pulled a paper from his jacket pocket, unfolded it, and announced, "Lenny Schick, I have a warrant here for your arrest in the murder of Leon Bratz."

And the place went wild.

Chapter 66

"Well, that went well," Cora said.

Chief Harper stared at her. "Well? I just arrested a man on no grounds whatsoever."

"You had a warrant."

"Yes, and do you know where I got that warrant?"

"I handed it to you."

"Yes, you did. When closely examined that warrant turned out to be a takeout menu from the Thai place."

"They have good curry puffs."

"I'll be sure to order them when I get my one phone call from the lockup."

"Who's going to arrest you, Dan Finley? You worry too much, Chief."

Henry Firth burst in the door. "What the hell happened?"

"Hi, Henry. Where were you? You missed all the fun."

"I was at the ball game. I thought with the suspect in custody and not talking, it

369

would be a fairly safe night to get away and see a game. The Yankees won, by the way, in an extra-inning thriller. So I was having a real good time until I hear on the radio driving back that Chief Harper served an arrest warrant on Matt Greystone's agent. Which is quite a surprise to me, because as county prosecutor I like to have a little input on arrest warrants. Particularly when they're arresting someone for a crime for which I already have a suspect in jail."

"That must be embarrassing," Cora said.

"I almost drove off the road! The only thing that kept me from calling you on the phone was it's against the law in Connecticut, and with my luck I'd get arrested, too! How would that look in the paper? Me getting arrested at the same time as the suspect?"

"I assure you everything's all right," Cora said.

"Oh, *you* assure me? How can everything be all right? I've got two suspects under arrest for the same crime."

"Technically, you've got one under arrest for the murder of Amanda Hoyt, and the other under arrest for the murder of Leon Bratz."

"That's even worse. Two killers? Acting in concert? *Not* acting in concert? What's your

370

theory here?"

"I think you'll be able to let Don go," Cora said.

"Oh, you do, do you?"

"I would think so. Surely someone planted the gun in his car. Even the stupidest killer wouldn't be so dumb as to hang on to the gun."

"He was drunk."

"You say that now. You'll sing another tune when you try to prove premeditation."

Henry Firth put up his hands. "Stop it. I'm not in the mood. Chief, what in the world possessed you to arrest Lenny Schick?"

"I told him to," Cora said. "I gave him a piece of paper. I said it was a warrant. It might not have been."

"You didn't look at the paper?"

"You're missing the big picture, Henry. You've got Lenny Schick in jail. He thinks we have him dead to rights. Actually, we haven't got a thing, but he doesn't know that."

"When he finds out, he's going to sue us for false arrest. And that charge will stick. You have any idea how much money that's going to run us?"

"He's not going to sue us for false arrest."

"Oh, no? What evidence did we arrest him

on, tell me that? What evidence did you have?"

"Oh," Chief Harper said.

"You didn't, did you? Not one thing. You arrested him on her say-so. She told you it would be all right, and things have gotten to the point where you believe her. Just because it's worked in the past doesn't mean it's going to work out now. We have a bad situation here, a very bad situation. Lenny Schick wants a lawyer. Is Becky going to represent him?"

"There's a conflict of interest. He's waiting for a lawyer to drive up from New York."

"When that lawyer gets here, we're toast. He's going to start screaming probable cause, and we don't have any. Or do we have some sort of probable cause you just neglected to tell anyone about?"

Harper sighed, shook his head.

"Great," Henry Firth said. "So what do we do now?"

"It seems to me there's only one thing that lets everybody off the hook," Cora said.

"What's that?"

"He's gotta confess."

CHAPTER 67

Dan Finley let Cora Felton into the conference room.

Lenny glared at her. "I'm not saying anything without a lawyer, and I'm certainly not talking to you."

"I understand why you'd feel that way. It's going to be awhile before you get a lawyer. Becky Baldwin can't represent you without Matt and Jackie's permission, and that may be hard to arrange. So you're going to have to get someone up from New York, and that'll take time.

"But here's the situation. You're going to get a very advantageous plea bargain. I can't say specifically, I'm not an attorney, but trust me you will. The prosecutor has no wish to do Matt Greystone any more dirt than he has to. You're going to cop to a plea of killing Leon Bratz, a sleazebag who was hounding your star pitcher Matt Greystone, and would not stop hounding him even after an injury had driven him out of the game. No one will blame you for that. Legally, you'll be guilty, but most people will see you doing the world a public service.

"Unfortunately, there's Amanda Hoyt. That's the hard part. Of course you had no choice. You had to kill her because she saw you do it."

Lenny stared at her.

"Yeah, I know. That's not true, but the truth isn't what's important here. So, say she saw you, and that's why she had to go. Doesn't make you the best person in the world. But consider this. A killer can't profit from their crime. They can't collect insurance. They can't inherit.

"But an agent? Whole different ball game, if you'll pardon the allusion. Matt's your client. You have a big commission coming. You still will if he continues to pitch. Which he will, if he's let alone to rehab. Will he ever be as good as he was? Who knows? But he'll get a shot.

"You and I have a mutual goal. We want Matt Greystone to continue pitching for the New York Yankees. That can only happen if Matt is allowed rehab and returns to his fighting form.

"I don't know anything about broken bones. But I know something about broken hearts. And I know Matt can't pitch with one, and wouldn't want to.

"The important thing here is that the truth doesn't come out. We gotta sell our version of the truth. Or rather, you do, because no one's going to believe anything I say. It will take a confession just to get people's attention.

"So, Amanda Hoyt saw you kill Leon Bratz, and that's why she had to go. Short, simple, effective, people will buy it. Then we don't have to get into any messy side issues like crossword puzzles that have you driving off the road.

"As far as that puzzle is concerned, Leon Bratz put it in the stove. You don't have to say you saw him do it. You don't have to mention it. All you have to do is not contradict it. Leon Bratz must have done it but you don't know when, and you have no idea what it means. You'll get away with that because Matt Greystone's brakes were checked and came out clean. Just another stab in the dark by Leon Bratz that came to nothing."

Lenny Schick blinked at her. "I don't understand."

"You don't have to. I do, and I'll help you through it. All you have to do is go along."

Cora took a breath, sized Lenny up.

"We're at a crossroads here. You have the choice of killing the goose that laid the golden eggs, or taking one for the team.

"You'll do some jail time, I'm not going to say you won't, but you'll get a shot, too.

"So, here's what you have to do, and here's what you have to say."

CHAPTER 68

"In a stunning development, in what the media has dubbed the Matt Greystone murders, Lenny Schick, Matt's agent, earlier today, quietly confessed to the crimes.

"Lenny's motive for the murders was the same one that led him to confess. A desire to spare his star pitcher publicity. Leon Bratz, a second-rate gossip columnist, who had made a career of smearing star pitcher Matt Greystone with leering innuendos, was unwilling to let even heartbreaking tragedy derail his blistering attack. Even as Matt Greystone, struck down in his prime, retreated from the spotlight, Leon Bratz followed him to Bakerhaven and prepared to crash the party. He had already begun a smear campaign in his columns intimating that Matt Greystone's calamitous car crash might not have been entirely accidental.

"Confronting Matt in his new home during his inaugural party, Leon came armed with a puzzle of his own construction, hinting at the illegitimacy of the car crash. He hoped to plant it where it would be discovered and delivered to the Puzzle Lady, who was a guest at the party.

"He never got the chance. Lenny Schick, unaware of the puzzle, but aware that Leon was up to no good, lured him to the sauna, ostensibly to discuss a payoff to cease his smear campaign. Once inside, confronted with the mocking face of Leon Bratz, in which there was no remorse, Lenny Schick could not resist the urge to seize the stone from the top of the stove, and bring the vermin's vile life to an end.

"Lenny deeply regrets the murder of Amanda Hoyt, but she had seen him enter the sauna and knew that he was guilty of the crime.

"Confession appears to have been a huge weight off his shoulders. The man is clearly wracked with remorse.

"I have here Matt Greystone, who wishes to make a brief statement, and then, per agreement, will take no further questions.

"Mr. Greystone, the sympathies of Channel 8 go out to you."

Matt stood quietly, waiting for Rick Reed to subside.

"I am deeply saddened by what has happened. Lenny Schick has been a dear friend since the beginning of my career. I am deeply sorry for what he has done. I know he felt he was acting in my best interests. I wish he had not, but I will not abandon him now. Though I personally will take no part in his defense, I have hired an attorney to act in his behalf, and any resources I have will be available to aid him in his time of need."

CHAPTER 69

Cora sat down across the dining room table from Matt Greystone. From the young pitcher's expression, *he* might have been the one who just confessed to two murders, instead of his agent.

"Let's talk turkey," Cora said. "You haven't been married as many times as I have, so you're not as good at lying. I can help you a lot. Your agent told a good story. I helped him with it, because he wasn't that good at telling stories, odd for a man whose career relies on hype. But then you've been his only athlete, and he hasn't had to hype you.

"You must know a lot of what Lenny said wasn't true. I know it wasn't true, because I made it up. Because I'm a Yankee fan who'd like to win the World Series, and I think you have a shot. Depending on how bad your arm is messed up, of course, but that's not my department.

"Anyway, let's talk about the puzzles."

Matt frowned. "Puzzles?"

"Confused by the plural? I mean puzzles, because there was another one. I suppressed it, you know why? Because Leon Bratz didn't make it."

"I don't understand."

"You find that odd, that he made one and not the other? It's not that odd, because Leon Bratz didn't make either of them."

"What are you talking about?"

"There was another puzzle. A puzzle presumably sent to you. A puzzle that said 'check his files.' The puzzle was untitled. Then, just in case I missed the point, another copy of the puzzle came titled 'Matt.' Oddly appropriate, don't you think? A puzzle to be named later?

"That puzzle answered the big question. Why did you come here? I mean, nothing against Bakerhaven, but what's it got going for it?"

"I had to rehab."

"Yes, but you could rehab anywhere. Why here? Well, in New York City you had access to Amanda Hoyt's office. In a country rehab, not so much. Unless, of course, you choose the town where she lives. Easy enough to slip away and see her at home. Which you needed to do. Because Amanda

Hoyt was your therapist. She handled your emotional problems. And I know you had several. Not the least of which was making the jump from unknown to star in the wink of an eye. A Horatio Alger story. *Do and Dare. Strive and Succeed.* I don't know if those are actual titles, but you get the gist. Poor boy makes good through tenacity and hard work.

"Then Leon Bratz takes aim. A few carefully worded stories hinting at your wife's prior relationship with your best friend. If only he'd let it go at that, but, no, you're on the road a lot, and your wife has lunch with your friend, Don. Nothing clandestine about it. I'm sure you knew. I'm sure she told you. But Leon Bratz showed you how it would look in print. You didn't like that, and you paid him off."

Matt said nothing, averted his eyes.

"Bad move. Worse than you could imagine, because you're really a babe in the woods. But the cover-up is so much worse than the crime. Absolutely nothing wrong with your wife having lunch with your friend. A very tiny story, no one cares. But you paying money to hush it up, suddenly it's a *huge* story and *everybody* cares. Now you have to pay to keep *that* story out of print, and the hits just keep on coming.

382

"Then Leon Bratz finds your wife's pictures in an old magazine. Or at least someone that looks like your wife. Close enough that it might have been her. And how much would you like to pay to suppress that?"

Matt kept his head down, stared at the tabletop.

"What's amazing is you managed to pitch well throughout all this. Which you did. And the better you pitch, the more your value increases. You sign a multimillion-dollar deal.

"Unfortunately, Leon Bratz has a sideline. He's a bookie."

Matt flinched. He looked up at Cora with wounded eyes.

Cora nodded. "Yeah, I know. Everyone and his brother bets on the Yankees when you pitch. But if you lose, and if Leon Bratz has taken the money everyone bet on you to win and bet it all on you to lose, he has a veritable goldmine. It doesn't have to happen every game. Just when he tells you to."

Tears ran down Matt's cheeks.

"For someone like you, a moral, all-American boy, it's a killer situation. There was only one way out.

"I don't know how you managed to break your arm. Did you break it first, before the accident? It's all right, you don't have to tell me. But somehow or other you did. And then you were off the hook. You might still have to pay money, but no way you'd have to throw games."

Cora paused, in case Matt wanted to say something, but the young man was too overcome with emotion to comment. "It must have been a terrible burden to carry," she said sympathetically. "For someone who's been married more times than you can count, let me give you a hint. You should have let Jackie in on it. She's true blue.

"Jackie suspected what happened. She hinted around, but she wasn't going to confront you on it. Couldn't get into your shell. She knew you were seeing Amanda Hoyt. She wanted to know why. Wanted to know those inner secrets you would not share.

"When you moved here it did two things. It told her Amanda Hoyt was really important, and it gave her a chance to find out why. She broke into Amanda Hoyt's office and stole her memory card. It told her nothing. The woman wasn't so indiscreet as to leave electronic files lying around. Her patient files were under lock and key.

"Jackie wasn't about to risk breaking into the house again. She wanted someone else to do it. So she made up a crossword saying, 'Check his files,' and slipped it to me at the fairgrounds, hoping I'd solve it, and break into the house. I'm not saying I did, but the hard files were broken into the night of the fireworks, and Amanda Hoyt suspected why. She gave Chief Harper a file folder to fingerprint, and there's every indication that file folder was yours.

"As for the other crossword. The police theory of the case. That Leon Bratz composed a crossword puzzle saying 'check his brakes.' Indicating the foul play caused your accident. That someone sabotaged your brakes so you would go off the road.

"Nothing could be further from the truth. Leon Bratz didn't create the crossword, and no one sabotaged your brakes. Jackie made up the crossword because she wanted me to check into your accident. Hoping I would share it with her and ultimately with you. No one sabotaged your brakes. You drove into a large tree. Jackie suspected that, and that's what she wanted me to find.

"Jackie had the puzzle with her at the party to give to me. When she walked into the sauna and discovered the body of Leon Bratz, she made a snap decision: let the puzzle be his. Otherwise it would be lost in the shuffle. Who could possibly care about a crossword puzzle with a murder investigation in full gear? Unless, of course, the puzzle was part of the investigation.

"So she stuck it in the stove. It was a bad move on her part. She wanted me to examine the car and find out nothing was wrong. Because that was the secret of your car accident. Not that anything caused the crash. The fact that nothing had.

"For Lenny, the puzzle was the last straw. Lenny was the little Dutch boy with his fingers in the holes in the dyke. He's already killed to cover things up, but here's a crossword telling people to poke into your accident. He does the only thing he can think of to divert suspicion away from the thing he fears most.

"He cuts the brake hoses on your car, gets into it, and drives it off the road. It doesn't have to be an accident, the car doesn't have to be damaged at all. It just has to go off the road so he can report stepping down on the brakes and nothing happening. The mechanic will check it out and see that the brakes are cut, people will think the crossword was referring to that.

"None of this is coming out. Lenny's taking the hit to make sure that it doesn't. And you and Jackie are disappointing Judy Douglas Knauer and giving up the house and moving out of town. And then, if your arm can mend, you can go back to pitching for the Yanks.

"You see why the confession's important? I know you'd like to have Becky Baldwin mount a ringing defense and save Lenny from the clutches of the law. That is not to be. For any number of reasons. Least of all, he actually did it. But it's not to be because it solves no one's problems. Least of all, Lenny's.

"Lenny needs you to be a success. It's the only chance for *him* to be a success. You're his only athlete. You're his bread and butter. More than anything else, he wants you to go back to pitching. Without the impediment of Leon Bratz. Lenny's paved the way for you to do that.

"I don't believe he was thinking like that when he struck Leon Bratz down. At the time he was just protecting you from him. But once the deed was done, there was suddenly so much more to protect you from.

"Who could have spilled the beans? Who knew of your obsession with Leon Bratz? Amanda Hoyt, of course. She had doctor-patient confidentiality, but people were trying to get into her files. And in a murder investigation, how far did doctor-patient confidentiality go? From Lenny's point of view, just the admission that you were *seeing* a therapist could be bad. If news of the relationship got out, including God knows what you might have told her about Leon Bratz — well, Amanda Hoyt had to go. And having killed once, the second time was easier.

"And that's why he killed her. Not because she saw him murder Leon Bratz.

"So, much as you want to protect Lenny, there's a limit as to what can be done. He's made his move by confessing. You can help him most by not making waves, and accepting the solution that he's put forth.

"Trust me, Becky will go to bat. The man will get the sweetest plea bargain that ever came down the pike. One that allows him to continue as your agent, even from in jail. And *that* is the supportive move that affirms more than any other your faith in Lenny Schick. You stand by him, keep him on as your agent, in spite of everything."

Matt looked up at Cora with pleading eyes. "So tell me. What do I do?"

Jackie Greystone came in the door. "Talk to your wife. I already have. She knows what has to be done. She'll stand by you, Don will stand by you, the Yankee organization will stand by you. And you move away to someplace nobody bothers you and you can actually rehab."

Cora smiled. "Then maybe the Yanks can win the damn pennant."

Chapter 70

"Couldn't we get closer?" Jennifer said.

"Closer?" Aaron said. "These are the best seats in the ballpark. You can't get any closer than this."

"That man is," Jennifer said, pointing.

"That man is an umpire," Sherry said.

"What's an umpire?"

"He guards the first-base line," Cora said, "and says whether a runner is safe or out and whether a ball is fair or foul."

"I wanna do that," Jennifer said.

The Yankees had expressed their appreciation of Cora Felton by giving her four field-level seats between first base and the dugout for a Sunday-afternoon game. Cora was in heaven, and not even Jennifer was going to throw a damper on it.

"Mommy," Jennifer said. "Tell them I wanna be an umpire."

"That's Aunt Cora's department," Sherry said. "This is her party."

"Auntie Cora?"

"You have to go to school to be an umpire. Do you want to go to school?"

"Pew-hugh!"

"Oh, now you're souring her on school?"

"I'm not doing anything," Cora said. "On the other hand, Jennifer is now going to think that all seats at the ballpark are this good. I have to tell you, for a girl brought up on the bleachers and the left-field upper tier, this is pretty damn classy."

"Cora said 'damn.' "

"I also said 'classy.' "

"Is that a bad word?"

"Only if you take away some of the letters."

"I can't believe any of your husbands didn't get you good Yankee tickets."

"Some did. Some didn't. I didn't stay married to them long."

"When is the game over?" Jennifer said.

"When the last man is out," Aaron said.

"It ain't over 'til it's over," Cora said.

"That's dumb."

"No, that's Yogi."

"What's Yogi?"

"Yogi was a Yankee catcher. He said funny things."

"Like what?"

"Oh, like déjà vu all over again."

"What's that mean?"

"No one's quite sure."

To a sudden roar the players ran out onto the field.

Jennifer sprang to her feet and cheered.

Cora beamed proudly.